WHEN ROOSTERS FLY

A NOVELLA BY

VAL DUMOND

When Roosters Fly
© Copyright 2012 by Val Dumond
This is a work of fiction. All the characters and events portrayed in this novel are either fictitious or are used fictitiously.
All rights reserved, including the right to reproduce this book, or portions thereof, in any form, without the express permission of the publisher.

Published by Muddy Puddle Press
P O Box 97124
Lakewood WA 98497
www.valdumond.com

ISBN 978-0-9679704-9-3
First Edition
Printed in the United States of America

Library of Congress Cataloging-in-Publication Data:
Available from publisher.
Dumond, Val
WHEN ROOSTERS FLY
An original novella, based on the screenplay "Harmony's Hope"
by Val Dumond
English/Val Dumond
Alphabetic order by last name
ISBN 978-0-9679704-9-3
1. Family. 2. Aviation. 3. History. 4. Pacific Northwest.

OTHER BOOKS BY VAL DUMOND

NONFICTION

Are You Singing Your Song?
The Anarchist's Guide to Grammar
Grammar For Grownups
Elements of Nonsexist Usage
Just Words — The Us and Them Thing
SHEIT — A No-nonsense Guidebook
to Writing and Using Nonsexist Language
Doin' the Puyallup
Steilacoom's Church
Olympia Coloring Book

FICTION

Sugar, Spice, and Stone
Ahlam's Stories
How We Fought World War II
at William T. Sherman Elementary School
Mush On and Smile (a novel)

ANTHOLOGY

The Sun Never Rises
Dream Makers

"When my mama borned me,
my daddy wrapped me
in a blanket and
whisked me off for a ride
in his airplane.
I've been flying ever since.

—Hal Harmony

When Roosters Fly

© 2012 by Val Dumond

"Yes, this is Harmony Airfield," the pilot called to his passenger, "the place where that loony guy crashed his plane when he tried to fly across the Pacific Ocean. Didn't even get off the ground."

The small high-wing Cesna circled the grassy airfield slowly. It looked like a short runway, and flat. A few small planes lined one side of the field, a hangar alongside. The small administration building sported a makeshift tower, from which came landing instructions into the pilot's ear.

The crackling earpiece shifted as the pilot strained to hear his instructions. Did he hear right? "Watch out for the baseball game on the west side; kids, and you never know what they'll do."

The plane descended toward the small grassy airfield-turned-baseball diamond, and easily rolled onto the short cement runway. The game in progress halted long enough for the children to watch the landing, then return to the suspense of the tied-up ninth inning.

"Granddad, it's my turn next, but Tanya hasn't had a chance to bat today… Granddad?"

"Humph."

"Gran, are you still watching the plane?"

"Naw, don't recognize it." But Hal Harmony was sure the plane carried the reporter who wanted to interview him about the crash. "Damned nosy-bodies," he muttered. "Why can't they forget? It's been fifty years!"

"What'd you say, Gran?"

"Sorry, kiddo. You wanted…"

"Tanya. Can she take my place at bat?"

"Okay, Melee," the grandfather/coach answered, turning toward the bench and yelling, "Hey Tanya. Take your turn next. Batter up, Grasshopper!"

The awkward skinny girl of nine picked up a bat as two of the young boys protested the switch. "It's not her turn," they complained. "She can't hit… the team is behind… put me in, Coach."

Tanya rolled the bat in the dust and looked at Grandpa Hal. She had called him that since the first time she met her friend's grandfather.

"Cool it, Grasshoppers," Coach Hal pretended to scold. "You know how it works. Everybody gets a chance at bat. How's she gonna be a good player if she doesn't get her turn?"

"Yeah but…" the boys began.

"Yeah but nothing. She bats! Melee, bring Tanya around tomorrow afternoon and we'll practice with her. Okay?"

Melee smiled her thanks at her grandfather and patted Tanya on the back to push her toward the batter's box. "Sure, Granddad. Thanks. Who knows, she may be the world's first girl to play baseball in the majors… after me, that is."

"You never know." Hal Harmony returned to his coaching position, leaned over and tugged on a blade of grass. He watched Tanya swing wildly at the first ball. She let the second ball go by — a strike —then swung at the third, missing it.

"Good try, Tanya," he yelled as she walked sullenly back to the bench. To his granddaughter, he called, "You're up, kiddo. See? You get another turn at bat anyway. Go get 'em. Knock it out of the park."

Melee grabbed her bat and stepped into the box. She let the first one pass. Someone in the bleachers called, "Go for it, Harmony. It's all yours. Go for it, Harmony."

Melee swung at another ball before she connected with the next. Hal watched the long fly ball spin up, up, up. At the top of its flight, the ball turned into an airplane in his eyes and he watched it dive, climb, turn and roll. It looped and played in the air. *That's the way we used to fly.*

The children's shouts dissolve into adult voices and Hal Harmony, a 20-year-old, dressed in a leather flight suit and helmet, makes his way through a crowd of well-wishers. He approaches his plane, "Harmony's Hope", and climbs into the single cockpit with all the confidence of a baseball player going to the plate. The young man is ready to start the longest over-water flight ever attempted by man.

The improvised Lockheed Vega sits perched atop a jerry-rigged wooden ramp at the end of the runway, ready to take off. The young Hal waves at the Movietone News cameras, then at the crowd of friends and well-wishers before he straps himself into the open cockpit and signals the start of the propeller.

He revs the engines and listens to the sweetly ticking Wasp as he fastens his goggles in place and, with another wave, releases the brake. The plane, heavy with its load of fuel, slides easily down the ramp as Hal teases the throttle forward, slowly gathering speed.

Those who stand close can see the smiling Hal, his face cooled by the morning air that rushes past him. Grateful for the chill, he presses the throttle all the way to the dash before he feels what seems at first like a sprinkling of cool water. He wipes a glove across his face, and sees the black gook that is spattering the windshield.

"Damn!" he mutters, leaning out of the cockpit to peer around the shield, only to be greeted with another dash of gasoline on his goggles.

With tail down, the fuel has bubbled from the tank breathers atop the fuselage in a steady spray, fogging Hal's view ahead. Desperately, he brushes back the goggles, but the stinging spray of gas is blinding him. Hal feels the ship wobble from the runway, swerving to the left, then the right. When the right wheel crumbles on the rough ground, the wing follows.

Without panic, Hal turns off the ignition, waiting for the plane to crash. He fully expects to die bravely in the explosion and fire that he knows will follow. The tanks contain more than 900 gallons of fuel.

Instead, the laboring plane slows down, veers to the side, and within moments the fuel-loaded Lockheed plows into a low embankment and lands on its nose in a cloud of dust. Hal's body lurches forward at impact. No explosion. No fire. No brave sacrificial death. Not even an injury. Only a smashed plane and a dirty face with humiliation written all over it.

As masses of screaming spectators converge on the wreckage, the young pilot jumps clear of the plane, rolls onto the grass as he was taught, and sits up to contemplate the disaster. He couldn't feel more devastated. His dream to be the first to fly the great Pacific completely wiped out, for the third time. Three strikes, he knows, means the end of the dream, his moment of fame shattered.

"Nobody to blame but myself," he calls to the crowd. "I can do it if they'll give me another chance."

"Too bad, Hal," he hears from a friendly voice in the crowd.

"Too bad, Hal." It was Melee's mom, Toni, who was consoling her father-in-law's lost baseball game. Hal needed a moment to collect himself back into his future. He smiled wanly at Melee, who rushed to grab his hand.

Tanya skipped up from the sidelines and joined her friend. "We'll win the next one," she said. "I'll try to do better next time."

"Come on, Granddad. It's all over. We lost… again."

"Say what?" Hal recovered from his time distraction. "Lost? I didn't know you knew that word. Just didn't win this one. There's always another at-bat if you want to take it." He raised his voice and turned to his team of Hoppers. "Playing the game, that's what's important — win or lose. Next time! Nice game, Grasshoppers! You all did fine. Everybody get a chance at bat? Good. We'll take 'em next time. Keep practicing. Keep 'em flying."

He held up his thumbs to the team and high-fived Tanya. "Hey Tanya, report for batting practice tomorrow at four."

The team scattered to pick up the gear and place the bags in the waiting van that belonged to the parents of the equipment manager. With shouts of "What's for dinner?" and "Let's stop for pizza," they drove off.

"You're a good coach, you know that, Hal," said Toni. "And a good father to Chuck too."

"Mom, can Tanya come home with us? Her mom didn't get to the game today."

Toni hugged her daughter with one hand and pushed back a strand of hair with the other. "I'm not going right home, Melee. I have to wait for Dad over at the office. We'll call her mother from there." The girls skipped off, headed across the airfield.

Hal and Toni walked slowly across the field, discussing the game. Hal's arm rested easily across Toni's shoulder. He was content that Charles had made a good marriage.

"Chuck's always telling me about the days when he grew up here. I often wonder how you managed. All those kids by yourself."

"Raising kids isn't hard if you stay out of their way," he answered. "Besides you get cheap labor. With my kids, I got help with the airport as well as the dish washing."

"Are you hinting we should give you more grandchildren?" Toni patted Hal's hand and was silent for a few steps. A new thought struck her. "Gee, Hal, I thought you had a convention or something to go to tomorrow. Are you sure you can work in batting practice too?"

"Oh rats, you're right. Oh well, I'll just be sure to make it home by four. If I don't, would you mind just pitching a few to Tanya and keep hoping?"

"Easy for you to say. I never played ball as a kid. Come on, Hal, race you to the hangar." She took off at an easy jog.

"Are you kidding? Running is for grease monkeys. By the way, when are you and Charles going to give Melee another Grasshopper to coach? Any plans?"

Toni caught the tease and returned, "Run, Hal, run. It'll clear your brain."

"Sorry, I don't run. Go ahead if you want. I'll meet you at the office."

Toni turned and, running in place, called out, "Did you see that plane come in... just before the last inning? May be a new customer for you." She turned to catch up with the girls.

Oh yes, Hal had seen the plane and also the portent of what most likely awaited him. A local plane, probably transporting another nosy reporter from Seattle. Most likely in town for the

Northwest Aviators Conference. *Take a deep breath, buddy, and you'll get through this,* he told himself.

Hal puffed into the office a few minutes later to find Toni sitting near her husband's desk. A quick scan of the room told him the reporter wasn't there.

Toni fidgeted with her car keys as Charles Harmony completed a phone call. Friends always told her how lucky she was to find such a neat appearing and efficient man to marry.

Efficient indeed. Charles had been around the airport all his life. He grew up there, knew little else. He flew in Vietnam for a short time toward the end of the war, but hadn't thought much of doing anything else since. Now he runs the office at Harmony Field for his father, doubling as airport controller. He loved the place, its faded pictures of planes tacked here and there on the walls, a work desk cluttered with his papers and a telephone, a makeshift computer desk, and a small table strewn with airport leaflets.

Doodle-do, a Rhode Island Red rooster, followed Hal into the office. The old bird, a descendent of the old chicken ranching days, had become Hal's pet. Old Doodle-do's forebears roamed this office when it was a combination chicken coop and slapped-together home for the Harmony brood. The home was replaced with a coffee shop when aviation picked up after World War II, but the chickens kept producing breakfast for the Harmonys for many more years.

"Silly rooster. God played a joke on you, Doodle-do. Great wings, yet the fool bird can't fly." Hal pretended to pet the bird, then plunked himself onto a chair.

Charles finished his phone conversation with "Yes, I wrote down the number. Eighteen. Yes, I'll tell him…. Sure, I'll let him know. Eight o'clock. Fine. Yeah. Okay," and slammed down the receiver. "Oh, hi Dad. That was the NAA Office. You have Booth Eighteen and you can set up your display after eight in the morning. Got it? I hope you don't need me until later in the day. I have a pile of stuff to do here in the morning."

"Nah, I can handle it okay. Not like I haven't done it before. Eighteen, huh? Hope it's a good location. We could use some new business, couldn't we, Charles? What do you want me to hand out?"

"Oh, you decide, Dad," Charles said absently as he leafed through the papers on the desk. "You know what we got to offer. And yes, we could use more business. When Air Tech pulled out last month, we were left with a gaping hole in our budget, if you know what I mean."

"Leave it to me. I'll find us some new customers."

"Make them paying customers, if you please," Charles chided. "And Dad, can't we do something with that chicken? Toni, where's Melee?"

"About time you noticed your wife, Chuck," Tony piped up sweetly. "Melee's over at Hal's apartment practicing baseball, I imagine. Are you ready to leave? Tanya's coming along."

Charles shrugged. "Yeah, okay. I'm about ready. Dad, the chicken. Please. Get it out of here. And tomorrow, be sure you get there early enough to set up before the convention opens."

"That's a rooster, Charles. Doodle-do is a *rooster*, not a chicken." Under his breath, he muttered, "No wonder you have only one child."

Charles closed his briefcase and headed for the door as his father called out, "Don't worry, son. Bright and early! I'll be there…" He turned away and added, "…when I'm damn good and ready."

BOOTHS 17 AND 18

"NOAH! NOAH, LET'S GO. WE'RE GOING TO BE LATE. It's nearly eight. How many times have I told you, the early bird gets the best spot."

Meg Webster was flying around the hotel room, pushing aside wet towels and clothes on the bed to reach the boxes she was checking. "We've got to make a good showing to find out how much business we can count on. If it weren't for your in-laws living here, Tacoma would be the last place on earth I'd consider. It's a far cry from California." Meg went on and on about the business, closing a large box, marking it, and kicking it toward the door.

"Noah, have you got enough wire for all the model planes? And don't forget the wire shears."

"All here, Mom," he replied, as he carried in a box from the other room in the suite. "How many times have we done this?"

"My, don't you look suave. Is that a new suit?"

"I got this one expressly to wear at these conventions. You gotta look smart to get the business. Isn't that what you always tell me?"

"Have we got everything?"

"Look, Mom. All here. Planes in this box; handout literature in that box; wire, shears and other miscellaneous stuff in the other box. All neat and ready to go. Did you call a taxi?"

"Oh, how could I have forgotten?" Meg joked, lifting a limp hand to her forehead. "Poor addled me…"

"I knew you'd remember. Just wanted something to say to calm you down."

"The cab will be downstairs before we get there. Come on."

Noah carried the big box of airplane models and his mother carried the smaller boxes as they left the room.

HAL HARMONY TOSSED BROCHURES and applications forms into a box, which he threw into the back of his pickup. He added a big sign that read, "See Harmony's Airport Display at the 1982 Annual Northwest Aviation Association Conference."

Next to the pickup sat Hal's plane, a two-seater blue and white single-engine Cesna. When he finished loading the truck, he walked over to it and called to the rooster that was pecking about the ground under the plane. "Okay, crawl in. You still haven't got the feel of what it's like to fly."

He started the engine, mentally ran through his check list, and taxied to the runway. He talked easily to Doodle-do as the plane took off. "See, we roll along this field of yours, then we pull back on the stick and… there, we're in the air. Feel it, chicken? Feel how light everything is up here?"

Doodle-do wiggled a bit before it began to peck about the seat to find the crumbs of somebody's potato chips, completely oblivious of being in what Hal called "the air".

"Stupid convention. Why did I ever agree to do this exhibition thing? At least I'll have a few minutes up here before I have to leave. The old pickup'll get me there in no time. Nothing can reach me up here. Look, Doodle. There's Mount Rainier, and all those other mountaintops and foothills and… there's the ocean. Mountains, sky, and water. In short, peace."

Hal regularly took a spin in the clouds after breakfast. He needed to keep adding time in the air, but he also had to keep adding freedom of the air to his spirit. To him, flying was like a morning hymn. He guessed he had flown just about every day of the 70-some years of his life. It began with trips into the sky with his father, even before he could walk.

"It always looks different up here, Doodle. Will I ever get tired of flying? You'd love it too, if you only tried."

The rest of the flight was quiet, Hal enjoying the air and Doodle-do enjoying the potato chip crumbs.

Headed back toward the airport, Hal mumbled, "But… I have to find a way to 'pick up new business'," he mimicked Charles. "I could fly like this forever, but I've got to head to that convention. Down we go. Now wasn't that exhilarating, Doodle-do? Don't you wish you had wings and could do that… wait… you *do* have wings. Why in blazes don't you use 'em?"

SEATED IN THE TAXI, the gear stowed in the trunk, Meg settled back for the ride to the convention center. She loved to gripe; it calmed her down. "I hate staying in hotels. It's so impersonal. Breakfast on a table with wheels and not a decent bowl of granola in the place. When I went for my jog this morning, everybody opened doors for me like I was helpless. Ye gods, I ran five miles. You'd think I could open my own doors."

"Cool down, Mom. We'll be back in a place of our own soon. Ellen is coming up this weekend and we'll look for a house with an attached apartment. You might even want to housesit for her parents when they take their winter Colorado hiatus."

"Hiatus, huh. People winter in Arizona or California, not Colorado. Don't these Washingtonians ski their own mountains?"

The taxi ride was shorter than expected, and Meg exhaled noisily as they drew up to the exhibitors' entrance. They quickly retrieved their boxes and headed inside.

As they dragged their boxes into the exhibition hall, Meg breathed another sigh of relief. "Good, we beat our neighbors," she observed as they approached Booth Seventeen. "Help me move this divider just a bit, Noah."

"Oh Mom, we don't need extra space."

"Just in case we do. Come on, give me a hand."

When they had expanded their display area, Meg and Noah unpacked the boxes and began to hang up model airplanes on wires that fell from the faux ceiling they had ordered special. Each plane was an exact replica of its larger relative. Painted with bright colors, the display began to look more like a collection of shiny balloons. Noah had placed the company logo, *Webster Classics*, above the doorway to the cheery display.

About a half hour later, Meg's attention was drawn to a man entering the hall in grand style. In a loud voice, he greeted some old friends. His voice became louder as it neared Booths 17 and 18, and Meg could see the white-haired old man smiling as he glad-handed old cronies. She continued to hang her models and pretended not to notice the intruder.

"Hey Mooney," Hal called out to a man walking by. "Isn't this space supposed to be ten feet wide? Looks more like only eight or nine. What the…" He spotted Meg and called to her, "Hey lady! Hey, you up on the ladder. What the hell you think you're doing?"

He could see all right. He could see the spider web of wires dangling from the lowered ceiling. He could see a young man, maybe in his thirties, and an older woman — *she's got to be at least 60* — on ladders, attaching model airplanes to the wires just above eye level. And he saw too that the divider panel had been moved, narrowing his booth and widening theirs.

Meg didn't answer right away. She coolly finished hanging another model before replying, "I'm hanging up model airplanes."

"I don't mean your dumb toys. I mean the wall of my booth. You moved it. You pushed it over until I don't have enough space. You can't do that. Can she, Mooney? I'm moving it back."

Meg pretended innocence as she coyly answered, "Oh, did that get pushed over? I'm so sorry. It must have moved when we were putting up the ceiling. Oh, please accept my apology."

"Well…" Hall recovered slowly. "It coulda been an honest mistake." He pushed the divider back into place, still grumbling. Which is why he didn't hear Noah whisper to his mother, "Mother, you know you pushed that wall over on purpose. You just told me that whoever gets here first can move things around to suit themselves. You know darned well…"

"Be still, Noah. The old coot'll hear you. And please don't call me *mother*."

"He's your age, Mom… er, Meg. Besides, everyone already knows I'm your son."

"It just doesn't sound businesslike. How am I supposed to appear like a serious businesswoman when my assistant calls me *Mom*? And besides, some people my age *are* old coots!"

"We've come a long way, Mmm… Meg. I really don't think our clients care what I call you. But if you insist, Meg it is."

"Hand me that gray Jenny, will you?"

The Websters continued to arrange their display area, attempting to ignore the monster in Booth Eighteen. Hal had turned on a radio, playing country/western music. Meg stared at him for a few moments before yelling over the music, "Not so much noise over there."

"What's the matter? The lady doesn't like music?"

"The lady likes music just fine, only not *that* kind."

Before she could get in another jibe, Noah had climbed off the ladder and picked up the gray Jenny. He whispered as he handed it to Meg, "Don't you know who that is? That's Hal Harmony."

Meg looked blank.

Noah continued, "He's the guy who tried to fly to Japan nonstop and didn't make it off the end of the runway! Back in the '30s. You must have heard of him."

"Uh, maybe I did, but I never thought he'd look like that. I've heard the story and always thought of Hal Harmony as a dashing young pilot. Why, he's a cranky old geezer."

"People grow up, Mom. They get old. Can you imagine what Earhart would look like if she were still alive? She'd be nearly a hundred."

"Sorry, son, Amelia will always be a young, tow-headed woman with a bright smile and endless courage. The thought of her growing old just doesn't seem right."

Somehow, Booths 17 and 18 were ready for the public that moved into the hall shortly after ten o'clock. Drawn by the spectacular display of pretty model planes, visitors crowded around Booth 17 to look at the reminders of early aviation.

Next door at Booth 18, an occasional passer-by would stop to pick up a brochure. Hal, a friendly sort, engaged them easily into talk about flying, about his concern with the disappearance of the small airfields, and the services that Harmony Field offered.

With all the activity of meeting old friends and making new ones, the morning passed quickly into mid-afternoon.

"Good heavens, Noah. It's nearly three o'clock and we haven't eaten lunch. Do you want to go for a bite?"

"Not just yet. I'm writing up this order. I think the guy will take a pair of these Wacos. Says he and his wife like to fly on weekends, but they go in different directions. Nice marriage, huh? Must have some kind of bank account to afford two planes. He'll bring his wife around tomorrow to give us the go ahead."

Meg left Noah to his writing and turned towards Booth 18. "Wonder what the old geezer did today."

"Mom, he'll hear you."

"I don't think so. He seems to be hard of hearing. I've been watching him. He nods a lot, like he's not catching all the words. And he plays that awful music so loud."

"I thought that all early pilots used to have hearing troubles from the noise of the engines in those old planes. Yours doesn't seem to be all that bad."

"Because I take care of myself. I use earplugs when I fly." In a gesture of mock friendliness, Meg hailed her neighbor. "Mr. Harmony. Pick up any business today?"

"Yeah, I did pretty well. Leased a few new hangar spaces. Picked up a few of your yuppy people who fly just for fun."

"Is there another reason to fly?"

"Well, no, I meant… hell fire, lady, you can't even carry on a short conversation. Maybe if you took some time to fly yourself…"

"Why Mr. Harmony, I've been flying since I was nineteen."

"You don't say. I'll bet you test flew all those old planes too, didn't you?" He pointed to the models floating overhead. When he noticed her face fall, he added quickly, "Sorry, just kidding."

But Meg was ahead of him. Very pleasantly, she answered, "Not the originals, Mr. Harmony. But I've test flown the replicas I make… all of them."

"Whoopdedo!" Hal knew when to quit. As he scanned the Webster models, he spotted one that looked familiar. "Hey, there's a Taylorcraft, just like the one I learned on. It's even the same color. I flew a green one just like that." He spotted another familiar shape. "And there's a Vega like… what do you do with these things anyway?" Maybe Mrs. Webster wasn't as dotty as he thought.

Noah handed him a brochure. "We build them."

"Oh, model airplane builders. Do you ever make them to fly by remote control?" Hal was having fun again.

"No, Mr. Harmony," Meg answered coolly. "Webster Classics does not build toy planes. We operate a bona fide business in Sacramento, where we build real planes, classical replicas of the real thing. You want a green Taylorcraft like you learned in? We'll build one for you." When she saw Hal's scowl, she added mischievously, "If you want a Lockheed Vega like the one you crashed in, we can build that too."

Oof, that hurt. Hal was indeed stopped in his tracks, his mouth open, his head cocked to one side as he looked at Meg. "Lady, I might just ask you to do that." And he walked away to cool off. *Who's she been talking to?*

When he returned, he found another crowd gathering at Booth 17, struggling with the temptation to touch the colorful airplanes that danced before their eyes. He heard bits of their nostalgic words.

"Ooh, that brings back memories…"

"I remember that one."

"That's just like one I saw when I was a kid."

"I flew one of those at the start of World War II."

PRACTICE MAKES PERFECT

HIS OWN MEMORIES FLOODED IN as he stood in Booth 18, his eyes wandering back to the Vega and his earlier days. For the first time, Hal was reminded of the reporter roaming the conference halls. What would he tell him? How can he explain to a stranger when he can't define his own feelings to himself?

He stared at the swaying little green plane and watched it grow into the full-size plane of his past.

> *The young Hal stands amid the disarray of the*
> *wrecked plane. He and his financial backer, Mr.*

Nicholas, argue as the gruff older man chews on a cigar.

"Come on, Mr. Nicholas. We know what went wrong. It's the tilt of the fuel line. Remember that it was the wheel that broke. They substituted a tail wheel at the last moment and that's what made the gas bubble up. We can go back to the conventional skid. With that fixed, I know we can do it. I know I can get off the ground easier and make it nonstop to Japan."

"But a five-thousand-mile trip takes two weeks. You guys are crazy to think you can do it in two days. I must have been crazy to put up my money on this hootenanny idea of a couple of boys."

"We planned. You know how we practiced takeoffs with heavy loads. We just have to improve the gasoline tank feeder lines. A little work on a new plane and we'll be ready to go in a few weeks."

"Sorry, buddy, but you're not listening to me. I'm out of money, and you're out of a backer. Now, you'll have to excuse me."

"Excuse me." Meg raised her voice and repeated, "Excuse me, Mr. Harmony."

"You're excused," Hal answered softly before snapping out of his memory. "You're excused. What do you want?"

"We've struck a lull at last, and wonder if you would keep an eye on our booth while we go for a sandwich."

"Can't. I'm leaving myself. My son should be around soon. Maybe he'll watch your toys while you're gone."

"Sorry I asked."

"Yup! Got to work out my baseball team." Hal turned abruptly and walked away, his nose pointed importantly toward the sky. *What nerve. I'm hungry though. Maybe I can pick up a burger on my way back to the field.*

Hal slammed the door on his pick-up, revved the motor for a few seconds, then tore out of the conference center parking lot. "Gotta turn my head toward those kids," he said to the dashboard. "Danged creepy woman!" He couldn't dismiss the woman in Booth 17. *Wonder if her son is as nasty as she is.*

As he pulled into Harmony Field, Hal could see Melee and Tanya waiting for him across the way. He grabbed his coach jacket and rushed to join them. "Why ain't ya practicing?" he yelled as he approached.

"Waiting for you, Granddad," Melee yelled back. "It's past four."

"Couldn't be helped; I have a life, you know. Now, Melee, pitch a few to Tanya. And Tanya, lower your shoulders when you hit, and straighten out the bat when you swing."

"How do I do that, Mr. Harmony?" Tanya pleaded.

"Like this." Hal stood behind Tanya and held her arms, gently guiding them in a swing at a make-believe ball. "Just watch the pitcher and keep your eyes on the ball. With a little practice, you'll know when it's time to swing."

Three missed pitches later, he walked back to Tanya and repeated the swing. "Think of the ball as coming right where you want it and swing horizontally — like this." He took the bat and showed her what he wanted her to do.

"What's hoor-iz-ongally, Coach?"

"Um, point your bat at Melee over there. Yeah. That's it, straight across, like you were balancing a nickel on the bat. Now try it again."

He counted ten tosses from Melee, then hollered, "Switch places. Tanya, get used to pitching the ball and let Melee bat. Ten swings, Mel."

Coach Hal retired to the bench and watched the girls take turns tossing and swinging at the ball. Doodle-do crawled out from under the bench. Hal absentmindedly began to stroke the rooster. That seemed to calm him down, in a way.

Within minutes he is back sitting next to his ruined plane, all those years ago, his head in his hands. An Old Friend approaches. "Sorry, Hal," he says. "This about wipes out your dreams of Japan, doesn't it?"

"Not quite. I'm sure Mr. Nicholas will back us for one more try. I know we can do it the next time. That's just a fuel problem; we can lick it."

"But the next time didn't work either, did it, Grasshopper."

"Naw. Even you getting badly burned on that try didn't stop me. I'm sorry about that, Old Friend, but a lot of us took our knocks. They were pretty exciting times, you gotta admit that."

The Friend breaks in, "Not so exciting for me."

"I'm thinking about Lucky Lindbergh flying alone across the Atlantic, Wiley Post flying around the world, Amelia Earhart setting records for women. We all took chances. We had to or we wouldn't be searching the galaxy out there today."

"Yeah, but the money ran out. Remember that last trip? Hal, remember the trip we started from Japan? You and me? We shipped the Emsco over to Japan and took off from there."

"Nearly made it too, Friend. Nearly made it. Got almost fifteen hundred miles out before we had to turn back. Nearly made it."

"That was a long time ago, Hal. And you're still thinking about it?"

"That's 'cause I plan to try again."

"Man, you're like that baseball player that struck out in the last inning of the Series game. Ya know, he lived his whole life waiting for another chance at bat!"

"Don't you worry, Old Friend. I'm going to get another chance at bat. I know it. One more chance."

"Granddad, do you want a chance to bat? We'll toss you a few if you want to take a turn." Melee stood before her grandfather and handed him the bat. Hal shook his head to dismiss the vision of his old flying partner.

"Nice of you, kiddo, but this is practice for you and Tanya. I'll throw each of you three more, then I have to go. Gotta go to a fancy NAA dinner tonight. Suppose I oughta change clothes."

"Oh, Granddad. You always look so handsome when you get dressed up. Can I help?"

"Wait a minute! I can still dress myself! So, I'm not handsome when I'm not dressed up?" He grabbed the bat from his granddaughter and took a couple of swings at the air before handing it back and heading to the mound. "Batter up!"

The girls enjoyed hitting the well-pitched balls. Melee hit two and Tanya almost connected with one.

"Good practice, Hoppers. You're looking better." To Tanya, he called, "S'long, Slugger."

"Yeah, Coach. See you tomorrow, Melee."

"Bye, Tanya." She took her grandfather's hand and told him, "You seem blue today, Granddad. Is something wrong?"

"No darling, nothing special. My memory's been jogged lately and I'm mulling some things around in my mind. I think it's playing tricks on me."

"Your flight to Japan?"

"What are you, a mind reader? Yea, as a matter of fact, yeah. It's been fifty years. How'd you guess?"

"You have the same far-away look you get whenever you talk about that flight."

"Do I talk about it? I wasn't aware."

"Sometimes. Remember, during my flying lesson the other day? Are you going? Do you think you'll ever make the flight?"

"Honey, that was years... no, decades ago. For me, this thing is like an unfinished dream. You know, like when you wake up fast and you're in the middle of a good dream that isn't finished? It kinda nags at you. Like you got something you have to do. Something that isn't finished... yet. Do you ever have dreams like that?"

"Yes. I guess I do. Like I'm going through Disneyland and then I'm not. Then Mom calls and it's time for school and I can't find my way back."

"You got it. That's the feeling. Well, I keep thinking about that flight, and the anniversary is reminding me that it isn't finished yet. Been considering another try." There, he'd said it aloud.

"Then I think you oughta do it. You know, like you always tell me, 'Just do it!' You aren't doing anything else. Dad takes care of the business and the Hoppers can get along without you... for a few days... if you have to go now. The season is just about over anyway. Why don't you, Granddad? Why don't you make your nonstop flight to Japan?"

"Aw, Melee. Melee. It's too late. This dream is over and I have to wake up and realize it's too late."

The two walked quietly the rest of the way back to the hangar — Amelia Jacqueline Harmony and Harold Hampton Harmony. Melee's father, Charles, greeted her with a hug and off they trundled towards home. Hal trundled off to shower and change and talk himself into enjoying the banquet.

DINNER WITH MEG

TWO HOURS LATER, HAL WAS SHUFFLING toward his assigned table as he spotted Mrs. Webster from Booth 17 heading in the same direction. Ye gods, she was walking toward his table. And woe added to woe, they were seated next to each other. Neither seemed happy about it, yet they regarded each other with indifference.

"And how is your baseball team, Mr. Harmony?" Meg Webster asked politely, prepared to make the best of it.

"They're doing just great. Do you like baseball, Mrs. Webster?"

"Ms. Webster, please," she corrected. "Or better, Meg... just Meg."

"Okay, Meg-just-Meg. Is that short for Margaret?"

"Actually, Marguerite. But I've always been Meg. And yes, I like baseball. Don't get enough chances to go to games, but I enjoy an occasional evening watching baseball when I can. Where does your team play?"

"At my airfield. I built a diamond for 'em at one corner of the field and we play Tuesdays, Thursdays, and Saturdays... sometimes. We practice whenever their parents let 'em come over to play." Hal smiled mischievously.

"I take it these are not grown men."

"Oh drat, you caught on. No, they're nine to twelve-year-olds. Some are girls too. They're called Harmony's Hoppers... Grasshoppers, get it? We haven't won yet, but we're planning to one day soon."

Meg smiled civilly and began to eat her salad. Others at the table took up their forks and worked silently on the greens for a few minutes. "Tell me, Mr. Harmony…" Meg began.

"Hal. Short for… Hal."

"Tell me… Hal-short-for-Hal, about your trip to Japan back… when?"

"My trip to… oh, that. I never made it to Japan, flying."

"But I thought… I heard…"

"Nope. Tried three times and struck out all three. The first time, a wheel buckled under the weight as we loaded the plane; it was ruined. The second time, my friend, one of the test pilots, cracked up the plane. The third time, I ended up in a mud hole at the end of the runway, the durned engine flinging gasoline all over the place. That plane was ruined too."

"You gave up after that?"

"Nope, we tried it one more time, flying backwards… well in a way. We started in Japan. Made it about a third of the way before we had to turn back. Took a co-pilot on that one. We flew a double-engine Emsco with a cabin, and we had fumes trapped inside, enough to kill us both. It was a nice boat ride to Japan though." He looked up to see the other diners at his table raptly following his story, forks frozen in the air. "And back," he continued. Nice boat ride back." He grinned at the diners and returned to his salad.

"So you quit after the try from Japan?" a fellow asked from across the table.

"Not by choice. The war got in the way, and… other things. I'm still planning to make that flight… one day… maybe soon." Hal's eyes lit up and took on a far-away glaze before he shivered with his new thought. The fellow appeared to make a penciled note and Hal's eyes caught the movement. "You a reporter?" You are. You're the guy that flew into my field yesterday."

"Sorry?" the man returned. "No, I'm not a reporter. Just another pilot." He returned the note and pencil to his pocket.

Hal tried to smile graciously, then remembered where he was going with the conversation and returned his attention to the woman beside him. "Tell me, Ms. Webster... Meg... were you serious when you said you could build a plane just like the one I... I crashed?" *My god, what am I doing? I haven't talked about this to Charles or even thought it all the way through.*

Meg mistook the glaze in Hal's eyes as the pain of remembering, and she knew how much it hurt to dredge up old memories. "I'm sorry, Hal. I shouldn't have mentioned..."

"Why not? I don't even think much about it anymore. At least until I saw your Taylorcraft today. And the Vega... just like Earhart flew and like one I tried to fly. Then I got to making plans in my head again. Maybe this time..."

"I didn't realize. I guess I thought you had forgotten it all. That was so long ago. What happened *after* the war to keep you from flying to Japan?"

"I got married. I had Marie and then the kids to look out for. But she's been gone a long time and the kids are grown up. Now I have time to think about doing it again." Had he actually said that aloud? "You know," he went on, the glaze returning to his eyes, "I might make it this time. I'm getting the feeling I finally might make my nonstop flight across the Pacific." He was beaming as he swept his arm toward his table mates.

"Then you never considered giving up flying? You've just postponed the trip?"

"Hell, I couldn't give up flying, ever. That's why I turned that chicken ranch and landing spot into my own airfield after the war. I remember the exact day. Some guy flew over my place, landed in my pasture, and asked if he could tie down his plane while he looked for gasoline. I was in business."

An aging pilot at the table added, "I remember those days of hopping around the countryside in planes we practically made ourselves. "We had to land any place that looked flat."

Hal nodded. "Yup! I could see into the future that day. We called it Harmony Field and did quite a good business when word got around. But… things seem to have slacked off lately. Price of gas, I guess. Or maybe folks are too busy to enjoy flying just for the fun of it."

Meg pushed back her salad plate and turned to Hal. "How powerful the memory must be to stick with you all this time."

"Ah, no. Some days I don't even think about…" He continued to tell his story as scenes of the third crash flashed through his head. The black and white Movietone News film clips of the inglorious scene — the crushed plane at the end of the runway, the astonished crowds, Hal's lost dream.

Hal finished his story and turned again to Meg. "No, I can't forget. Can you really build a Lockheed Vega like the one I had? *Just* like it?"

"Why yes. That's my business. I've been building old planes for years. Real ones. Planes you can climb into and fly… up in the air." She was teasing Hal now.

"How'd you get started? Did your brother build models? Or your son?"

"That's a very sexist remark, Mr. Harmony."

"What do you mean 'sexist'?"

"You're supposing that only boys build models — my brother or my son."

"Oh well, I just assumed…"

"Exactly. You assumed. As a matter of fact, I built model planes *before* my brother even tried. He found out quickly that he couldn't do it well, so he quit."

"How old were you? You don't look that old."

"What a nice thing to say. Actually, Amelia was my role model. I wanted to be her when I grew up."

"A lot of women were flying back in the thirties."

"I wasn't one of them. Not old enough. But I built models so I'd know all about planes if I ever met her. Then Amelia disappeared and I kept hoping she'd come back. She never did."

At that moment, Hal saw something that had escaped him earlier. Meg looked just like Amelia — tall, well-toned body, short-cropped hair, bright shining eyes. The others at the table were well into their dinner as Hal and Meg got acquainted, their own dinner plates untouched.

Meg heard more of Hal's story of building a business out of a chicken ranch, adding a café to feed visiting pilots, an apartment to house his family, and offering free airplane rides on weekends and holidays to friends and neighbors. He proudly added how he and his father had built their own airplane; most aviators did back then. And he told her about his three children, Amelia, Charles, and Wiley. "And there's Charles' daughter Melee, a nickname for Amelia, my only grandchild."

"All named for flyers of the early days."

"Oho, you noticed. Yes, you can say I was the equivalent of today's groupies… an aviation groupie."

Meg laughed.

"So, you *can* appreciate a little joke."

Hal learned that Meg earned her engineering degree after returning to college in the '60s with her son Noah. Both students at Berkeley, he studied music and art before switching to business management, and she became one of the university's first women engineering students. The age of feminism had hit California. "No, I don't smoke pot!" she told him.

"How did you learn to fly?" Hal asked.

"When I was 19, at the local airport. When we moved to Sacramento from Michigan, we lived near a small field — much like yours. To make my models more authentic, I looked for new ways to make them appear like the real thing. That's mainly why I learned to fly."

"Does your husband fly?" An innocent question for all appearances.

"He was an aviator and began dreaming of building a real airplane. We considered building planes after the war, but…"

She didn't get it. So Hal tried again. "He still in business?"

"He… uh… he flew with the Army Air Force during the war and was shot down just before it ended, a year after Noah was born."

"I'm sorry," Hal said, trying to collect his thoughts. "Is Noah here?" He looked around the room.

"These social things aren't his cup of tea," Meg answered. "He opted for a swim and an early night. I think he'd have preferred finding a jazz group to sit in with, but I don't think he'd find one around here."

"The early night sounds good, but I'm not a water person. So how did you work out at being a single mother?"

"I took the insurance money and went back to making my dream come true — building real planes that looked like my models."

"Hell, you've been doing this all these years and I never heard of you?"

"I have a small plant in California, Mr. Harmony. I only decided on this move to the Northwest a few months ago. Now I'm looking for a place to move my company. You can tell by the large attendance here that the Northwest is full of... uh... discerning pilots."

"Can you make a living at this, Mrs. Webster? I mean, does this pay the bills?" He didn't realize he was becoming formal again.

"Very nicely, Mr. Harmony."

"Hal, please."

"In the beginning, I had to give flying lessons and service planes to make ends meet."

"All this while you're raising kids?"

"Well, of course. But I have just one child — Noah. He isn't much of a flyer, but he's a good businessman. He sees that the bills are paid and I see that we have new business coming in."

"But you're a... a..."

"Careful. A... *woman*? Is that the word you're looking for?"

"I was going to say, such a small woman."

"Maybe that's because I talk too much instead of eating," Meg joked, taking a few bites of the smoked salmon on her plate. "I have lots of energy; I do yoga and I eat right. Gradually, I narrowed the business down to making replicas. And yes, to answer your question, Hal, it pays the bills very comfortably. Noah sees to that."

Hal too stabbed at the salmon dinner and finished a few mouthfuls before he returned to his question. "Meg, can you really build a Vega like the one I cracked up?"

"Yes, Hal, of course I can. But... why?"

Hal's heart was fluttering, not at Meg's attention, but from the hope that was growing in his chest. "I don't know you very well, but I have to tell you that I've been waiting my whole life to finish this trip. And I didn't understand that until just now."

They both laughed, again drawing attention from others at the table. Hal continued, "Things never seemed to get off the ground for me, never took off, so to speak." He grinned at his pun. "Still, I want to make that flight to Japan, nonstop, in my old Vega."

"But..."

"Just wait. I'm not finished. I'm seventy... er... something. I've spent my life dreaming of that aborted flight, hitting pop flies all my life. Nothing has worked the way I wanted to. But I'm going to try again. I have to!"

They finished their meal without another word, both deep in their own thoughts. As the evening program began, Hal reached over and whispered in Meg's ear, "Let's get outa here. Would you join me for a drink in a little bar I spotted next door?"

"Well, I should…"

"This doesn't seem like an evening for *shoulds*," Hal returned. "Come on, I'm buying. We have some more talking to do."

Trying not to be noticed, the two tiptoed to the door without breathing. Outside, the warm summer air embraced them as they strolled into the Trading Post Bar. The Mariners' game was on the television and only a few tables were filled. Most of the viewers were crowded around the bar. Jim Presley had just come to bat and Hal paused a moment to watch him hit a cool single.

"You really like baseball," Meg commented. "I hear it in your words as well as your attention."

"Sorry, I just love this Mariner's team — lots of potential this year." The two ordered — Cutty Sark neat for Hal, and gin and tonic for Meg. They found a table away from the noise.

"You seem sad, Hal. You said that nothing was working for you, but you have lovely children, so you must have a wonderful wife to go home to."

"Marie's been gone a long time, and the kids are grown. I kept hoping the business would grow, that Marie would come back, but the years passed and nothing changed. Now I have time to think about going to bat one more time for myself. Sorry, but the more I think about it, the more I believe I'm going to make it this time."

"Then your wife hasn't died?" Meg was fishing this time.

"I don't think so. I haven't heard from her. She left me and the kids some years ago. Took a plane up one day and flew off, just flew off and never came back."

"But your children. Surely they…"

"God, you really are reaching for excuses. I'm getting tired of excuses for me. The kids are out of my life — except Charles. He helps me at the airport. Wiley's a commercial pilot and Amelia…"

"Amelia. Is she the eldest?"

"Yes. Amelia lives in California. She and her husband run a fancy restaurant in San Francisco. I fly down there once in a while for a good meal." Hal paused before adding, "Yes, all my kids still speak to me. Guess I'm lucky there. But I don't think we're what you'd call *close*."

"I'm still fascinated that all your children are named after aviators."

"Well bless my Aunt Hepzibah, you're right!"

"Don't turn nasty again. You're really a fairly nice person. You like flying and you sound very proud of your children. That makes you a successful father. A *single* father." Meg couldn't help herself.

The two were beginning to relax over their drinks and had settled back in their chairs, Hal straining to hear the television. He sat straight up suddenly and asked, "How do *you* measure success?"

Meg, amazed at a philosophical question, took a moment to reply. "Doing something that makes you happy, for one thing. I love constructing replicas of old airplanes. Your airfield is still operating after fifty years. That says something about your success in business. Why would you want to ask that question?"

"My field is just about the same as it was when I started. A few hangars. Charles helped me build a pretty neat apartment in one of them, so I live at the field."

"Sounds like you're living a great life."

"Guess so." Hal hadn't thought about it that way. "Just got used to living on an airfield after so many years. My pet is a rooster who must be a descendent of one of my old ones; he thinks he owns the place and nobody has the nerve to get rid of him. Much like me, maybe. I don't know if I could live anywhere else."

"You're a strange man, Mr. Hal Harmony."

"Let me put it this way. I could own Sea-Tac Airport and still feel like I'm playing in the minors, as long as that trip to Japan remains unfinished. One of these days, I want to try it again. I didn't know that until I heard you say you could build my plane."

"There are many obstacles."

"Don't throw cold water. You woke up all my dreams and they've been hammering in my head all day. What would it take, Meg? What would it take to build my old plane for me?"

"It's expensive. Very expensive. I can't just order out for a Vega. Airplane manufacturing has changed a lot in five decades. We'd have to start from scratch: frame, fabric, engine…"

"You have the plans, don't you? You've done this before, and I can help with the work. I don't do much else around here."

"I'm not even sure we can get some of the materials… original materials. We… might… have to do with substitutes… and gas tanks… we'd have to make them ourselves, or have them custom made. They'd have to be just right."

"We'll build gas tanks. Whatever you need. If we could do it as twenty-year-olds, we ought to be three times as smart now. Good god, Meg, are you throwing up obstructions because you're testing me, or because you don't want to do it? You don't want to take on an old codger like me for a client?"

"And that's another thing. You're older now. Do you really want to make that flight? In an open cockpit? Without today's equipment? It wouldn't be easy for a younger man, but you..."

"My great Aunt Geraldine! You let me worry about that. All I need is the plane. Will you help me build it and outfit it for my trip?" Even he noticed how he called it "his trip", as if it were already a reality.

"Have you thought what your children will say? Will you let me install some high tech equipment, a canopy, a radio, upgrade it a bit — for your safety?"

"You sound like my kids."

"You might try listening to them. And we'll have to deal with the FAA. And the National Traffic Safety Board."

"Can't you see, I've delayed this trip for fifty years — the longest ball game in history. I know I have only one more chance at bat, and I want to take it."

"And if you don't make it, what if..."

"I strike out... again? I might get on base. But if I don't get to bat, I can't do either one." Hal paused, sipping his drink and looking at the ceiling. "Lindy hit a homer... out of the park," he said at last. "So did Post, although it cost him his life. Amelia flyed out. I need to finish my turn at bat, even if it means dying in the process. I want to make this flight..." he paused again, "...if it's the last thing I ever do. I mean that."

Meg didn't say another word. She sensed his determination, even as he doubted himself. Why not! Why shouldn't he have his shot at his dream… one more time. "You really are serious," she said after a few minutes.

"One more inning. Call it overtime. That's all I'm asking. I'll take my chances."

Meg drained her glass and set it down slowly. "Right. I'll pull out some plans as soon as I find a place for my shop."

Hal had been considering this one. He blurted out, "How about my place? You said you wanted a small field with access to a mainline airport. Come out next week after the convention and look at my place, will you, Meg?"

"Okay. I'll come out and look. But frankly, I'm not sure we could stand being around each other that much. You aren't the easiest person to deal with, you know."

"You ain't exactly Mother Theresa yourself. Talk about a pushy broad… sorry, *wo-man*," he said stressing each syllable. "I'll try if you will."

The two didn't reorder and left the bar. Hal drove Meg to her hotel in his truck and they shook hands amiably at the door. On the way home, Hal was reminded of the strange plane that had arrived just before the convention. Maybe it wasn't a reporter. Charles had identified the plane as a taxi from Seattle, carrying only one passenger. The pilot refueled and took off within minutes. Charles didn't see where the passenger went.

On the last days of the conference, Meg and Noah busily met potential customers and went about their business. Charles hosted Booth 18 most of the time and seemed unaware of his neighbors.

Hal popped in on the last day. When he approached his booth, Charles was talking to a pretty young woman wearing jeans and jacket, her hair in a ponytail. He stood back for a moment, waiting for them to finish, but Charles waved him over. "Hal, I want you to meet Cindy... er, what's your last name?"

"Benson. My friends call me C-B." She extended her hand. "Happy to meet you, Mr. Harmony. You are very famous."

"I am? Surprise to me."

"Oh yes, you're the pilot of that plane. Fiftieth anniversary coming up? Aborted flight to Japan? Bust-up on film? Remember?" She spoke to him as if he was in his dotage, unable to understand.

"Oh my god, Charles. She's the reporter. You've been talking to her?"

"Sorry, Dad. I didn't know. Are you sure?"

"Young lady, what do you want? Why are you talking to my son?"

"Oooh," cooed the young C-B. "I didn't know he was your son. I just thought he was a handsome..."

Charles blushed as he stammered, "We were just... I only said... she was asking... oh, I'm so sorry, Dad."

"You *are* a reporter, aren't you, Miss?" Hal took her arm to lead her away.

"Yes. I have to let you know that or I can't use what you tell me. I work for *The San Francisco Chronicle*. They want a story to go with footage they're copying about aviation in the '30s, and your name came up."

"Came up, huh? Just like that. How did it come up?"

"We were having lunch at a restaurant when the owner came by to greet her customers. Turned out to be your daughter. When she heard us talking about flying and famous pilots, she told us about you... your attempts to fly to Japan. My editor thought you'd make a good story. Can we talk some more?"

"Amelia! So that's it. No, we cannot talk more. I don't wish to discuss my life with any reporter, much less one who hasn't been on this earth long enough to know what real airplanes look like." Hal and C-B had reached the door. He continued to hold her arm as they went outside.

"Hey, I've had the bum's rush before, but not by an old washed-up guy like you. Maybe you don't merit a story."

Hal stopped dead still. "When was the last time you flew a plane, Miss... er... C-B?"

"I haven't ever flown a plane. In fact, I was flying with white knuckles on that dinky plane from Seattle. Not so much the jet from San Francisco. Why?"

"I fly planes. I have built planes. I understand what it takes to lift a machine of steel and wires off the ground. Yes, I wanted to be the first to fly across the Pacific in a single bound, but unfortunately, I am not Superman. Nor did he exist in 1933. I am human.

"It's not as if I didn't do everything possible to make it happen, the time was not right — apparently. Three tries and I struck out. I do not believe that makes a story. What might make a story..." but Hal stopped short. He wasn't about to announce another try, if there was to be one. He couldn't go through that again. *This project with Meg, if it happens, must be done in secret. Nothing for the press.*

C-B retrieved her arm and faced Hal with one last question. "Do you think anyone will ever fly to Japan nonstop in a small plane?"

Hal nearly smiled. "I'm sure it's already been done. Yes, I'm sure it's been done."

"Then you…"

"I am happy operating Harmony Airfield and watching my granddaughter play baseball. And that ends our interview… er, discussion."

C-B hailed a taxi and drove off. Inside the cab, she took out a pad and pen and wrote furiously all the way back to her hotel.

WELCOME TO HARMONY FIELD

FOR THE REST OF THE CONVENTION, Meg and Hal went their separate ways after spending hours at Booths 17 and 18. They didn't even sit together at the closing luncheon, although Hal couldn't help but notice how many interested people surrounded her.

Meg and Noah returned to California without further business discussions with Hal.

The week passed quickly. It was early afternoon when Hal heard the plane and spotted the shiny red Cessna circling the field. The landing was perfect. As the plane taxied toward the hangar, Hal walked out and waved. He assumed this was a new customer, the result of his work at the convention.

The pilot cut the engine and climbed out, jumping easily to the ground. She didn't need to remove her helmet before Hal recognized Meg. "Welcome! Welcome to Harmony Field."

"Nice little set-up you have here," Meg responded. "I like it. And it's so close to the city. I like that too."

"You had no trouble finding us?"

"No, your directions were perfect. You had talked about Harmony Field enough for me to almost feel as if I were coming home." Meg closed down her plane, then turned abruptly as she felt Doodle-do sidle up to her.

"Well look at that," Hal howled. "Old Doodle-do doesn't take to most strangers. And there he is, getting just as cozy as can be. Jumping jehosiphat. The old bird still..."

""Doodle-do? That's his name. A beautiful bird. Rhode Island Red, isn't it?"

"You know your birds, lady."

"Do you still keep many chickens, Hal?"

"Naw, just this one. Can't fly worth a darn, but he thinks he belongs here. Must be sixth or seventh generation, but he keeps hanging around."

"How old is he?"

"Nine, no ten years, I think. Thereabouts."

"I didn't know they grew that old. Average age is somewhere around five or six, isn't it?"

"Don't think Doodle-do knows about averages. His only problem is that he's been around planes and flying long enough, you'd think he'd be taking to flying."

"Roosters don't fly, Hal. Anybody knows that."

"I don't know that; I've seen 'em fly... not far, but fly. I think it's a matter of wanting to, and old Doodle-do doesn't want to. I take him with me when I fly sometimes, but he can't get the hang of it."

Meg laughed. "How about showing me around this place. I'm eager to see the layout. Show me what you got, Mr. Harmony."

The two walked toward a small hangar, Doodle-do at a safe distance, following Meg, checking her out. Hal pointed to a small building behind the main hangar. "That's where we used to raise chickens," he said. To the rooster, he asked, "Remember your home, Doodle-do? Over there is where the old café used to be. My kids grew up here, fueled the occasional visiting plane, fed the pilots, and helped 'em with plane repairs. Over there..." he pointed to the large new hangar,"...is where the planes of my new customers soon will be stored. Down this way is where you can build planes, if you want to."

They walked through the large bay doors of the hangar. "There's a good spot for Noah's office. Out here is a lot of space for a production team to work, and over there," he pointed to a corner room, "is your office, right next to the main hangar." Meg poked around, mentally placing her team and the equipment.

"Good," she said after about fifteen minutes. "I'll notify my team to prepare for the move. We may have to hire some new people if we get all the work we talked about at the convention. Meanwhile, I can look around for materials for your new... old... plane. We should begin looking at plans in a few weeks. Now, I have to call Noah and tell him that Webster Classics has a new home."

"Come over to my quarters and use my phone. I'll fix you a cup of coffee… or would you rather have tea?"

"Hot tea sounds good. I'm not sure if I can get used to Washington chill after living so long in California. When summer is done, it really turns cool fast here, doesn't it?"

"Most folks find the weather just right — not too hot, not too cold."

The walk to Hal's apartment was short and quiet, each with their own thoughts about what was happening. When Meg entered the comfortable, well-designed rooms, she was surprised at the balance. Not frilly, but not overly macho either. Bright NASA space paintings decorated the walls amid photos of children and airplanes. A cozy stuffed divan faced the fireplace, and she saw the small kitchen off to one side.

"Why Hal, this looks civilized. I wouldn't have guessed."

"My great Aunt Tilly! We-uns here in the woods still have an eye for the stars. We even have herbal tea" (he pronounced "herbal" with a strong "h") "if that's what you prefer. I keep it for Amelia, my daughter. Care for some?"

Meg, amused at Hal's contrived backwoods accent, answered, "*Erbal* is just fine." She moved toward a NASA photo.

"I've always looked at outer space as the ultimate flight," Hal told her.

"Don't ask me to build a space ship, Hal."

"You know what I mean. There's something about all that space out there that's fascinated me from the very beginning. I guess you could say I was born looking up. My daddy grabbed me soon as I was born and took me for an airplane ride, so I've been told. My folks always accused me of staring at the sky.

There wasn't much up there then except stars. Lindbergh and I were of the same era. I wanted to be just like him, do the same pioneer flying. I guess I just didn't have what it takes."

"You have something that Lindbergh doesn't. You're here. You have another chance."

"My, my! Are you crossing over to my side?"

"I didn't know we were opponents."

"We're not. But what if I still can't do it. What if you're just wasting your time on my dream. I'll look even more foolish than the last time."

"Maybe we ought not to even try it then. You struck out three times fifty years ago and now you're..."

"Whoa! Don't get me wrong. Sometimes I get to thinking about the way things happened, and sometimes I think I was afraid then. Too afraid to go through with it, like bailing out before I had the chance to find out if I could really fly."

"Of course you were afraid. We're all afraid of failing. We're all afraid of trying something for the first time." She smiled wickedly as she added, "But then, you tried it three or four times."

"Gad, you're a pain." Hal poured the hot water into a cup and handed it to Meg. "Can't resist the jabs, can you."

I'm not trying to be mean. You just scare me when you talk so seriously, when you express your doubts. I'd like to make this a fun project, something we can both have fun with. If it works, it works. If it doesn't, at least we can say we had fun. Can you work that way?"

"Yeah!" Hal's shoulders relaxed and he sat back in an easy chair. "In fact, I'd prefer it. You're right. I oughta get something out of this, even if it isn't a trip to Japan."

The telephone interrupted. Hal answered with, "Harmony Field... Sure I am... Sure I can, Mr. Janssen. You bet. I'll be there before noon tomorrow." He hung up and turned to Meg. "Sometimes I fly for this timber company. There aren't many pilots who can land planes in the middle of the woods like I can. Which means, I'll be gone for a couple days."

"Good, that'll give me time to get my people in California ready for the move."

A knock on the door was quickly followed by Melee rushing in and running to her grandfather. She wore her baseball uniform and looked flushed. As she hugged Hal around the neck, she excitedly related her news. "Tanya got a hit today, Granddad. She actually hit the ball. It rolled to the pitcher and she forgot to run, but... she hit it!"

"Great balls of fire, Aunt Mathilda! What a day, Melee baby, how's my sweet granddaughter?"

"I'm fine, Gran... oh, you have company."

"Just business. I'm sorry about leaving the game early. What's up? I'd guess that if you're here, that son of mine must be close by. Where's your dad?"

"He went over to the office. Said he'd be back in a few minutes. Can we go for a ride this afternoon?"

"No school?"

"No, Granddad. It's Saturday."

"So it is. And you've come for your flying lesson. I remember." Hal's head had been doing that to him lately —

flying off on its own. "Come over here, Melee. There's someone you ought to meet. Melee… Amelia… meet Meg Webster. Mrs. Webster makes model airplanes, only she makes 'em big enough to fly."

"Hi," Melee managed meekly. She wasn't used to strangers.

"Amelia. My favorite name," Meg replied. "I got started building planes because I admired your namesake, Amelia Earhart. Or am I just assuming you were named for a famous woman pilot?"

"Actually, I'm named for my Aunt Amelia. But everyone calls me Melee."

"So I hear." To Hal, she said, "Oh yes, your daughter… Amelia."

"She lives in California. I told you about her. She and her husband run a restaurant, a very famous…"

"He's not her husband anymore, Dad." Charles had entered the room and corrected his father. "They were divorced four years ago. Remember?"

"Well, he should be… married to her. They run a business together." Then he remembered his manners. "Meg, this is my son, Charles. He manages this place now that I'm *re-tired*." Hal stressed the word.

"Retired, my ass… eyeballs," Charles glared at his father. To Meg, he offered a polite handshake. "We met at the convention last week, and I admire your work. No, I'm afraid my father is not as retired as he claims. He flies more hours than I do and spends more time working on old planes than the mechanics do. By the way, Dad, there's a message for you at the office from Janssen's Timber. I guess they want you to…"

"Yeah, they called here a little while ago. I'll be flying out to Kalispell in the morning. Be gone three or four days." He took Melee's hand and winked at her. "And you'll take care of Doodle-do while I'm gone, won't you?"

"I always do," Melee said with a slight groan to her voice.

Meg stood up. "I must be going, Hal. I've enjoyed meeting your family."

"Oh, this is just a piece of them. We've got lots more."

"I look forward to meeting them." She caught a questioning glance from Charles and explained, "I've decided to lease part of that new hanger for my business… and the plane I'm going to build for your father. It…"

"The plane you're going to build… for my father?"

"I was going to explain this, Charles, but things have moved rather quickly. I've asked Mrs. Webster to build a plane for me." Hal shot a look at Meg across the room that told her to say no more. *I'm not going to tell Charles about his project just yet.*

"Can we afford it?" Charles asked.

"We'll talk about it later, son. I feel kinda nostalgic for the good old days. Actually, we're doing a trade-off. I'm giving her a deal on the space in return for her work on the plane. I'll pay for the materials and the work; we'll trade our profits."

Charles wasn't sure what to make of his father's explanation, but he was polite, if anything. "That's very generous of you, Mrs. Webster. I guess you have a solid market for those old planes. I see quite a few vintage planes coming in here lately. Maybe old planes are coming back." He remembered his father's derisive remarks about "that lady in Booth 17".

"Don't be rude, Charles."

"Yes, Charles, they are coming back. But now I must be going… and let Amelia get her flying lesson." As soon as she noticed Charles' surprised look, she amended her words. "Ride… Melee's ride."

"Did you forget to call Noah?" Hal asked.

"That's okay. I'll tell him when I get back to the hotel. Which reminds me, I need to call a taxi."

"I'll call for you. Where are you staying, Meg?"

"At something called the Blue Angel motel; they said it was close by."

"I can drive you back, if that's okay with you?" Charles offered.

"Fine with me. Thanks. Goodbye. Goodbye, Hal. Call me when you get back from… wherever… and I'll give you a progress report."

Hal managed a few hand signals behind Charles' back to warn her to say nothing more about their business arrangement. As soon as she and Charles were out the door, Hal grabbed the tea cups and rushed off to the kitchen, calling, "Get ready for your ride, Melee."

PLANE PLANS TAKE SHAPE

WHEN HAL RETURNED FROM MONTANA, his head was full of ideas for building his plane. But first he had to clarify his plans with Charles. Still, every time he approached the subject, he backed away. How could he tell his family he was going to fly nonstop to Japan in the same old plane that had nearly cost him his life all those years ago?

Meg and Noah completed the move of their business to Harmony Field just before the Christmas holidays. Noah and his wife Ellen, both skiers, insisted that Meg take time off to spend the holidays with Ellen's parents in Vail. Upon their return to Washington, they buckled down to hiring staff to replace those they lost through the move, arranging machinery, and beginning production for two planes that were ordered as Christmas presents.

Hal still hadn't confessed his plot to his family. Each day he meandered innocently over to the Webster Classics company to check progress and occasionally to help out. By February, the framework for his plane had been started; within a week, pieces of the fuselage were in place; by month's end, the fabric was added.

As they worked, Meg in overalls, the two conspirers maintained to everyone that this was a plane that Hal hankered for — and Meg was able to deliver. Their friendship grew as they took turns smearing goop over each other while they smoothed the fabric on the plane. They were having fun.

Charles stayed away from the hangar until his curiosity got the better of him. He walked over to deliver the propeller shipment, which was left at his office instead of over at the Webster hangar. He walked in just in time to overhear Meg ask Hal, "How long do you think it'll take you to get to Japan?"

"Get to where?" Charles bellowed.

"Oh, hello Charles," Meg greeted him. "I was… uh… just asking your father about the distance to Japan. He…"

But Hal knew the time had come to explain his dream. "I'm going to fly to Japan, in my old Vega." The last thing Meg heard as she quietly slipped outside was Charles response.

"Oh Dad. It's happened. You've lost your mind. No way! No way my eighty-year-old father is going to fly across the ocean in a cracker box with wings. You cannot be serious. You're kidding. Ha-ha! Good one. You're kidding... aren't you? You really had me going there, Dad."

"No, Charles, I'm not kidding. Hang fire, Aunt Miranda, why on earth shouldn't I go? And I'm not eighty, nowhere near. It wouldn't make any difference if I was eighty or ninety or a hundred." He paused for air. "Damn it, Charles, I don't need your permission. I'm going. It's important to me. I knew you wouldn't understand. I guess I thought when you saw what a great plane this is, you'd feel different."

Charles pointed to mounds of wood and paper and fabric stacked around the hangar. "This wouldn't have made it fifty years ago; it sure as hell won't make it today. The air traffic alone..."

"Charles..."

"I'll have you confined, committed, tied up if I have to..."

As the two men faced off against each other, Meg returned, drawn back by the noise of the argument. Both she and her red overalls looked grimy and tired as she approached, still holding a set of plans. "Charles, perhaps you and your father ought to simmer down before..."

"So sorry, Meg. I didn't know you were still here."

"Perhaps when you two are alone, when Charles has all the information, he'll feel differently."

"You condone this, Mrs. Webster? I thought you were a sensible woman, but... but..."

Hal interrupted. "Later, son. She's right. We'll talk later."

Charles, still fuming, stomped out, calling over his shoulder, "You bet we will."

"Well, Meg, isn't this fun? Never mind Charles; he'll come around. He's a sucker for old planes. He'll come round."

"Sure. He'll be all right when he gets used to the idea. I haven't told Noah yet either."

"Told him what? He must know you're building a plane for me."

"You know," Meg hedged. "I haven't told him I'd be flying across the ocean in a small plane."

Now it was Hal's turn to erupt. "Hells bells! You're not. Who said *you* were going?"

"I just assumed..."

"This is a one-man flight and I'm the one man who's making it. Nobody said anything about you going along. I'm not taking a woman with me. No. No. No. This is something I have to do alone."

"But what about a navigator? You said you had one on your last try. Amelia had one. You're not a young man anymore, Hal. Even if you're not eighty yet," she snickered. "Let me go with you, as navigator."

"No. I have to do this alone. If I go down, well, I'll go down... alone. Nobody can take your turn at bat for you. Batting is something you have to do by yourself. No! This is something I have to do... alone... myself."

"I appreciate that, Hal. But please, won't you reconsider? Think how much more fun it would be with two of us."

"Fun, fun, fun. Is that all you think about?"

"And I don't weigh that much," Meg continued, ignoring him. "I'd more than pay for my weight with navigation… and company. We'd have time to talk about the old flying days…"

"Heck of a lot of talking we'd get done in open cockpits at ten thousand feet with the wind blowing past."

"I'm enclosing the cockpit with a canopy. And we'll use the radio."

"A canopy? What radio? Those weren't in the plans. I'm not planning on radios and canopies; we didn't have 'em then. We'll do without 'em now. It wouldn't be the same."

"You have to have a radio, Hal. Flight rules have changed. You can't fly in and out of airports anymore without a radio. Do you want to have to turn around and fly home without landing in Japan? That's basic equipment. Some of those early long distance flyers had Morse code radios; you've got to be able to communicate."

Before Hal could catch another breath, she added sarcastically, "Ships at sea don't notice airplanes anymore. And they'd hardly think to radio your position to anybody if they saw you were in trouble."

"What are you trying to do? Build a nineties plane with the look of the thirties? There'll be nothing in my plane that wasn't there fifty years ago… and that includes you."

Meg knew exactly what to say and she said it. "Perhaps we ought to re-think our agreement. Perhaps you ought to find someone else to build your plane for you. Perhaps…"

"Now don't get your back up in a hissy fit. We'll work something out. We had a deal. You build; I fly."

Hal was pacing, thinking, trying to come up with more reasons or… could he concede something and continue his dream? After a moment he stopped, faced Meg, and said, "Maybe a little radio. I'd hate to go down on some remote island and be found the next day by some teenagers out cruising. But I won't use it unless…"

His words continued, aimed more at himself than at Meg. "My god, first this woman wants to ride along for the fun, then my son doesn't want me to go at all, now she wants me to fly a 1930 plane with 1980 technology. What next? She'll probably want to paint the plane pink!"

"Sorry, Hal. I don't paint anything pink. But that brings up a question. What color do *you* want to paint it?"

Drawn off topic, Hal answered, "Green was a jinx. You choose a color. Just so it ain't pink."

"How about yellow? Canary yellow. You know, like Earhart painted her first plane?"

"How'd you ever know that? Did you help her?"

"No, it's my business to know." She was delighted to see his sense of humor returning.

"Hell, I don't care what color it is. Yeah! Yellow's fine." Hal turned and walked away muttering, "Canopy! Radio! Canary yellow!"

NAVIGATOR OR NO NAVIGATOR?

RADIO OR NO RADIO?

BY EARLY MARCH, Meg was working on the interior of the plane. That morning she was wearing a new pair of brightly striped coveralls, her hair still rumpled, and her face tattooed with grease.

Somehow, Hal and Meg had avoided further discussion of Meg's accompanying him to Japan. They worked side by side with a strain between them that still didn't interfere with their teasing each other. Hal commented constantly about Meg's less-than-ladylike wardrobe, and Meg made insinuations about Hal's age. Charles remained completely aloof from them both. He had his own plans for this mad project.

When Hal entered the hangar one morning, he began, "How's it coming, Meg? Golly gee, it's beginning to look like my plane."

"Glad you came by, Hal," Meg called as she crawled down from the hatch. We've got to iron out a few things. We can't go any further without your input."

"What's the problem, Mrs. Webster?"
"The problem... Mr. Harmony... is threefold. Are you going to take me along? Will you agree to a closed cockpit? And will you approve the radio?"

"No kiddin'! We're that far?"

"Just about. We're ready to configure the cockpit. So do you want two in front? Or one behind the other? You recall how Earhart rode in between the gas tanks on her first crossing the Atlantic... as a passenger. I don't feel like riding between gas tanks."

"Sounds like you've decided you're going to tag along."

"Yep! Since we're sharing costs in this thing, I'm claiming part ownership and the right to go along." Meg sat down on a nearby barrel and crossed her arms, waiting.

Hal knew what lay ahead. He just didn't like this woman making his decisions. "My sweet Aunt Gertie! Okay, I'll think about it. You might be a good luck charm."

Meg relaxed her arms. "Well, that's decided. Guess you realize I won't work on this another minute if you don't let me ride with you."

"No, it's not decided. I said I'd think about it."

"Good. Put on your thinking cap. Side-by-side seating so we can talk? Or one seat behind the other?"

"You don't give up, do you! Hmmm." Hal leaned on one elbow and furrowed his brow. After a few seconds, he scowled as he said, "Okay, side-by-side... in case I decide to take a navigator, but room for one of us to go in the back if we want to."

"That may take some doing with the gas tanks back there. And, speaking of gas tanks, I'm having trouble finding them. They'll have to be made special, and I've called just about everybody I know; they're either too busy or they don't have the materials. I'm running out of possibilities."

"I know you. You'll bully somebody to build 'em for you; you always seem to get what you want." Hal turned to leave, took a couple steps, then turned back. "Hey, Mizz Meg. If you don't have plans for Thursday afternoon, bring your son and his wife and join us for my birthday party. We always have a big wing-ding."

"Your birthday is Thursday? I didn't know. Thanks." Meg stood up and headed back to the plane, calling over her shoulder, "I'll think about it."

Meg didn't need to think about attending the party. She cajoled Noah and Ellen, but they begged off, opting instead to start an early weekend with her parents. Thursday afternoon, Meg drove to the airfield with a feelings of apprehension that moved through her body like the first day of school or taking off to test fly a new plane. *Wonder if the family is as stubborn and single-minded as he is.*

Hal's family had gathered early that morning. Charles and Toni immediately donned aprons and headed to the kitchen where they began clanking pans around. The kitchen opened onto the living room where Hal sat with his daughter Amelia, sipping new wine and carefully talking around the subject of her broken marriage and their restaurant.

It was Amelia who guided the conversation away. "Daddy, Chucky says you've got a girlfriend who's building a plane for you and that you're going to fly off across the ocean with her. Sounds romantic. When do we get to meet her?"

"Hell's bells, Amelia. Chucky talks too much… about things he doesn't know."

"But Daddy, Chucky said…"

Melee, who sat across the room working on a model airplane, sensed her grandfather's discomfort and asked, "Hey, Aunt Amelia, are you going to stay awhile this time?"

"No, darling. Just the weekend. I have to fly back Sunday. Rob and I have a restaurant to run, and I don't trust him alone with it for more than a couple days."

"How come Uncle Rob didn't come with you?"

"Somebody has to keep the restaurant open. Tell me, Melee, have you met Granddad's girlfriend?"

"She's not a girl, Aunt Amelia. She's a lady, old like Granddad."

"Hey there, wait a minute," Granddad objected. "I'm not old; it's called *chronologically disadvantaged*. Tell your Aunt Amelia how you're learning to fly."

From the kitchen, Charles joined the conversation. "Learning to fly? What's that?"

"Oops," Hal muttered under his breath. To his son, he called, "Surely, you must have guessed. But there's nothing to worry about… Chucky."

"Enough with the 'Chucky', Dad! Answer my question."

"Granddad is teaching me," Melee confessed, proudly adding, "I got to hold the stick the other day. I can't reach the pedals yet, but Granddad says it won't be long."

"Rudders, Melee. Rudders. Not pedals."

"Oh yeah."

Aunt Amelia walked over to her niece and hugged her. "You have to keep growing, and that doesn't take any effort. You'll make it one day. I remember when I was your age, Dad…"

Oh please!" Melee moaned.

Now it was Hal's turn to rescue his granddaughter. "A little respect for your elders, Miss Smarty Pants. Tell me, Amelia, how's business?"

"Let's get back to the other subject, Dad. Who is this chick Melee mentioned? Anyone we know?"

Hal chose his words carefully. "The woman to whom Melee is referring is a biz-nezz acquaintance. She has leased one of the hangars for her biz-nezz and that's that!"

"Tell her about the plane, Granddad."

"Holy jehosiphat, girl! You've got the biggest mouth in the country."

"Well, tell her."

"Yeah, Grandad, tell me. What about the plane?" Amelia rose to refill her wine glass in the kitchen.

When Hal remained silent, Melee announced, "Mrs. Webster is building a plane for Granddad."

Hal faced his granddaughter. "Who told you that?"

"I heard Dad talking to Mom about it. He says you're going to fly to Spain or somewhere."

"Melee! That's enough. You're going to confuse your Aunt Amelia. We'll talk about this later when I can inform your young mind what is happening."

"Wait a minute," Amelia cut in, moving back to the sofa. "We'll talk about it now. This woman is building you a plane to fly to Spain? You're serious?"

"Oh for Pete's sake, no, Amelia. I promise you, I am not flying to Spain. Melee has confused something she heard and..." Hal stood up and headed for the kitchen. "Yes, Mrs. Webster is building a plane, but... Melee..." As he passed the table where Melee was working, he leaned over and whispered, "You're going to pay for this one."

Melee loved her grandfather and felt a certain understanding of him. She smiled her understanding smile and said, "Did I just hear a car drive up? Maybe that's… his girlfriend," she teased. "Er, oops, Mrs. Webster."

"Must be her now. I'll get it." Hal turned toward the door, avoiding Amelia's glare. But Melee was faster. Before Meg could ring the bell, Hal and Melee opened the door together. Hal gently pushed his way in front of his granddaughter and bent over to whisper to Meg, "Ixnay on the iptray! Not a word about the trip."

Meg looked a tad confused until she saw Amelia. To Hal, she replied in a loud voice, "I'm glad to see you too. Happy birthday." She handed Hal a brightly decorated package and added, "I'm sorry about Noah. He and Ellen are spending some time with her parents. Ah, this must be Amelia."

Meg smiled and held out her hand as she crossed to the sofa, at the same time waving to Charles and Toni in the kitchen. To Hal, she said, "She looks a bit like the other Amelia… very pretty. Is your son Wiley coming?"

"Wiley called yesterday to say he's stranded in Las Vegas. His flight ended there and… miraculously, he's socked in."

"He popped into the restaurant a couple weeks ago, Dad," Amelia recovered her bearings. "He looks okay; you don't have to worry about him." To Meg, she said, "I'm so pleased to meet you, Mrs. Webster."

"I just wish he were here. I like to see all my kids."

"Dad," Amelia began slowly, "let's get back to that trip. And, uh, there's something else we need to talk about — you and I."

"Hal handed Meg a glass of wine and explained, "Amelia is the mother of this family. She has to take care of all of us. We all check in with her and she checks on us."

"I understand, you need some time alone. Why don't Melee and I open your present and start putting it together? Then you and Amelia can talk."

"Oh yeah, my present. What'd you bring me?"

"Open it and see."

Hal tore off the wrappings and lifted out a model airplane box, a replica of his old Taylorcraft.

"Aw, you shouldn't have. Look what Mrs. Webster brought, Melee. This was my first plane, way back when. Many a pilot took his first solo in a plane like this. She says she'll help you put it together." Melee took the hint and gently moved a few pieces of the model she was working on to the floor in the corner. Hal leaned against the kitchen counter and watched the women in the living room get acquainted.

"And when you're finished, we can paint it green," Meg added. To Amelia, she said, "Hal told me you were to fly your own plane from California, Amelia. I should have guessed that Hal's children all would be pilots."

"Yes, you don't grow up at Harmony Field without knowing how to fly. We all do. Only Wiley went commercial. Do you fly, Mrs. Webster?"

"As a matter of fact, I do. And please, call me Meg."

"And you build them too? I got that much out of Dad." Amelia noticed her father straighten up, and she couldn't resist. "Now, about the plane you're building for Dad. Will he be able to fly it somewhere?"

"I suppose so. That's what it's for. Planes do fly, don't they, Hal?"

"Yeah." Hal nodded at Meg before he turned toward the kitchen and asked, "Hey Charles, Toni, how much longer till dinner?"

Before he got an answer, the telephone rang, and Hal picked it up. "Hello. Hey there, young fella. You still in Vegas? You couldn't be grounded in a better place, except how much fog is there in the desert? Never mind. I won't squeal on you. Yes, he's cooking, and I... we have company. Yes, she's here too. Thanks for the card. Got it yesterday. Ah, okay... thanks. Good to hear you too." When Melee ran to the phone, gesturing wildly, Hal added, "Melee wants to talk to you."

He handed her the phone and she started telling her Uncle Wiley about the baseball team and her friend Tanya. Hal joined Meg and Amelia.

"Any wife for Wiley on the horizon, Pop?" Amelia asked.

"Not that I've heard. Leave him alone. You're not the one here to promote marriage."

Melee handed the phone to her father and moved back to the table to unpack the new model plane.

"Was I promoting marriage?" Amelia sought help from Meg.

But Hal interrupted before she could answer. "Wiley's based in Houston, gets to California more than he comes up here. He..."

And Amelia interrupted right back. "Now, back to my other question: what's the plane for?"

Meg looked at Hal and remained silent. Amelia too stared at him, stony faced. All they heard was the sound of Charles' voice on the phone, "Bye for now, Wiley, fly safely."

Until Hal began slowly, "You might as well know. Meg's building a Vega like my old Lockheed, and I'm... I'm..." his voice dropped and the words spilled out rapidly, "...I'm finishing the trip I started all those years ago, flying to Japan."

Hal sat back and waited for the reaction. Which came like the first rush of wind before a spring thunderstorm. The first sound was the clap of thunder as Charles dropped a pan in the kitchen. Toni turned around to stare at her father-in-law. Melee looked up from sorting pieces of balsa wood, her senses telling her to remain quiet.

Amelia calmly set her glass on the coffee table and rose slowly. "Say... that... again."

"You heard me. I'm flying my Vega to Japan. Like a shoulda done fifty years ago."

"Oh, then you know that it's been fifty years. You're not hallucinating, thinking you're twenty years old again. You're not..."

"Amelia, I'm perfectly aware of what I'm doing. It's very simple. Listen carefully. I'll repeat: I am flying to Japan!"

"Over my dead body, Dad. You're... you're not young anymore. There are too many other planes out there for you to run into. It's a long flight and you're not up to it. This is crazy." Amelia paced the floor as she thought up more reasons. "Are single planes even allowed to fly over the ocean? Small planes aren't built for long trips. You'll get lost. The world is different than it was back then. Dad! This is simply crazy, out of the question." She closed her argument, unable to find more to say.

"Simple, yes. Out of the question, no, my dear child, and I call you that gratuitously. I am an adult, capable of making up my own mind." He shot a glance at Meg who smiled but held her tongue. "What I *will* do and what I *will not* do is none of your business. This is my decision. And this is something I… will… do!"

"Dad, you didn't tell me that." Charles had found his tongue. "I mean, I thought you were kidding. I didn't think you were actually going to… Dad, I agree with Milly. I don't think this is something you want to do."

"Oh, and you know what I want to do? Hells bells! Of course it's something I want to do, or I wouldn't be doing it. I don't see what all the fuss is about. You are my children. Like it or not, you have no right to tell me what I can and cannot do. Now buzz off! Come on, Meg, let's take a walk."

Before the two conspirators could reach the door, Amelia called out, "Dad, wait up. We have to talk… privately… for a moment. Meg, will you excuse us?"

"No. We have nothing to talk about," Hal grumbled.

"I believe we do. Dad, please. Not about flying. This is important."

When he saw the look on his daughter's face, he told Meg, "I'll just be a minute."

Meg returned to work on Melee's model airplane; Charles and Toni went back to the kitchen, and Hal and Amelia disappeared into Hal's bedroom.

Hal had planned his house very carefully, and this room was both his sleeping area and his private space. A pleasant, masculine room, it was large enough to have a cozy sitting area, complete with bay window that faced the airfield. Amelia steered her father to the armchair; she remained standing.

"Dad…"

"Good lord, Amelia. You look serious enough to… what's wrong? You can't be that upset about my flying to Japan. Is it Rob? Has he hurt you?"

"No, it's not Rob, not even Japan. Since this seems to be confession time, I have to tell you something. Actually, I'm bringing you a message."

"A message? Who from? Come on, Amelia. Out with it."

"It's… Mother. I mean… this is really bizarre… she's… she walked into our restaurant a couple days ago. Just like that, after twenty years and then, poof!"

Hal closed his eyes and lowered his head. "Marie? Marie?"

"Yeah. She just walked right in, out of nowhere."

"Marie? You're telling me that Marie walked into your restaurant? She's alive?"

"Yes, Dad. Mom's very much alive and very well. I almost didn't recognize her. I think she's lonesome and misses you. She wants to come up here. That's her message. She wanted to come with me today, but I thought I'd better prepare you."

Hal's head shot up. "Prepare? Yeah. Good lord, this is more than a surprise! Why'd you wait so long to tell me?"

"I didn't know what to say. I couldn't just walk in and say, 'Hi, Dad. Mom's back.' Anyway, she wants to see you." Amelia held her breath for a moment. "She wants to come up here."

"No!" Hal stood up and looked across the airfield. "No, out of the question. I mean, N-O! Have you told Charles?"

"Of course not. He'd fall apart. He's always missed Mom much more than any of us."

Hal's surprise had turned to anger. He paced across the bedroom, muttering, half to himself, "Why now? Why now? What the hell is she trying to do? Hasn't she hurt us enough? Now she wants to do it again?"

"She's older, Dad. Maybe she regrets what she did. I think she's having second thoughts."

"Second thoughts! Second thoughts! A hell of a time to have second thoughts! She should be up to two hundred thoughts or five hundred by now. Why, Milly, why? I'm at a loss for words." He sat down on the bed beside his daughter, the little girl who grew up to fulfill the duties of her missing mother. His arm curled around her shoulders and he could feel her body shake with the sobs welling up inside her.

Amelia was also at a loss. "I don't know, Dad. You'll have to talk to her to find out. She wants to see you."

"Milly, you talked to her. Did she tell you why? Why she left? How did you feel seeing her again? What did she have to say for herself?"

"Gosh, Dad, I was already with Rob in San Francisco when she left you. I haven't really missed her all that much. Except at my wedding... and at Christmas... and on my birthdays. She walked into the restaurant. I didn't recognize her until she called me Milly. Then all the memories came back." Amelia's eyes succumbed to the tears and she dabbed at them with her sleeve.

"Oh my god! I am so sorry."

"It's not your fault, Dad. Got some tissues?"

Hal handed her the box and patted her back helplessly.

"Yes, we talked. She said she's been living in... someplace in the South. She works part-time for a pilot's association. She tried a regular office job, but got bored. She lived with some guy for a while, but they've parted. She says she's been alone for about three years, and, she's getting on. Dad, I don't know why she left? She wouldn't talk about that."

By this time, Hal looked as if he'd been kicked in the stomach. His steam had been kicked right out of him. "I'm not sure myself, kiddo. She just flew away... and didn't come back. We argued about letting Wiley go to Canada to sit out Vietnam. Charles was already on his way to Nam and she didn't want to risk both boys. Wiley was her youngest. She was just protecting him, but we talked and talked, and she wouldn't give in."

"I remember you calling me to ask if she was with me. I couldn't believe she just walked out."

"Flew out, darling. She flew out. One afternoon, she took up one of the planes and never came back. I didn't reported her missing, just figured she'd come back when she was ready. Then the days and months passed and... well... she never did."

Amelia pushed back the tears and resumed her motherly role. "What matters now is that she's flown back into our lives. So what do we do?"

Hal made no response.

"When I saw her, it was like waking up and finding someone in your room. I was startled, but not too surprised. We talked. She wants to come back... where she belongs."

"No! Not on my great Aunt Fanny's life! No sir! No!" His voice was loud enough to be heard in the living room. Hal walked slowly toward the door, stopped, and turned around. "Let's not spoil the party with this. We'll tell Charles later, after dinner. I'm going to take Meg for a ride. I have to clear my head."

GETTING TO KNOW YOU...

THE TWO RETURNED TO THE LIVING ROOM. Hal grabbed Meg's arm and they headed for the door. Amelia watched them leave, then signaled Charles that everything was okay. Almost too gaily, she asked, "How long till dinner?"

Outside, Meg and Hal slipped into their jackets and walked into the aftermath of a brief Northwest rain shower. The runway glistened with the spritz as they walked silently toward the hangar.

"Kids. They think they can run your life," Meg said at last.

"They don't fool me. They'll come around. They like to throw their young weight around, almost as if to get back at us for all the years we engineered their lives. But they know I'm still the boss here."

"Sure. Noah does the same thing with me. Tries to tell me how much I can do, when to go to bed, and what I should do about this and that. He plays man-of-the-house with both Ellen and me. But I'm getting to an age when I want to be on my own."

"Oh come on," Hal teased. "Certainly, you're over twenty-one."

Meg laughed and returned, "Sometimes I still feel twenty-one."

They laughed together and walked without talking for a bit. Then Hal mused, "Family ties. More like family chains. I don't know much about your family, or Noah's."

For all the time the two had spent together working on the plane, they had not talked much about their families until then.

"Not much to tell. Noah's an only child. You know that. We both attended college... together; you know that. Well, I returned to college and picked up a degree; he met Ellen, and they married. No children, and Noah won't allow Ellen to work. They stick pretty close to her parents. I think Noah senses I'm pulling away; I've been his whole family all his life."

"You've never talked about his father... your husband."

"I met Wilson when I went to college the first time. The war was just starting and we both dropped out. Wil joined the Army and died just before the war ended, just before his twenty-seventh birthday. He'd been shot down and died of his wounds before they could get him home."

"I'm sorry, Meg. You've had a difficult life."

"I notice you don't talk about your wife. Marie? Is that her name?"

The two had entered the hangar and stood before Hal's plane, the fairly new blue and white Cessna. "Let's take a ride. Want to make a fly-around in my plane? The rain has stopped."

Hal opened the bay doors as Meg climbed into the passenger seat and secured the hatch. After Hal did an exterior check of the plane, he climbed in behind the controls. "Make sure that belt is tight, Meg. I don't want you to fall out."

"Nice try, Hal, but I don't think you're in a mood for kidding."

Hal taxied out to the runway, revved the engine, and took the plane into the air. Circling the airport, he seemed to regain control over the day's events. Yet, it wasn't until he leveled off at about 4,000 feet that he spoke. "I always think straighter up here. And besides, I want you in a place you can't walk away."

"Why would I do that?"

"Hmmm. You never know."

Hal took his time, maneuvering the plane through the clouds until the sun glowed brightly. "CAVU," Meg said as the sun surrounded them.

"I didn't think you'd know that term," Hal said.

"I told you I've been flying since I was nineteen. In fact, that was how I met Wil. He and I both belonged to a volunteer Air Search and Rescue in college."

"CAVU — Clear Ahead, Visibility Unlimited," Hal mused. "So much meaning. So appropriate."

Meg couldn't hear him over the sound of the engine, but she realized he was pensive. *That's a good word, pensive,* she thought.

"Oh hell, I don't even know why I brought you up here," Hal said at length. "We have nothing in common. You're a Democrat, for god's sake. Why should you understand what's going on?"

"The project? What does politics have to do…"

"No. Yes. Sorta. It's not the project. It's this family thing. Amelia's failed marriage has brought some issues back. I always wondered about Marie, my wife. Why she left. Why Wiley remains apart from us. Charles is the only one who's made marriage work. Why do they object so much to this flight?"

"They love you a lot. That's probably why they're so worried. They don't want to risk losing you... like they lost their mother."

"But that's not why I wanted to talk to you."

"No? Has something happened?"

"Yes, that's what Amelia wanted with me." Hal cleared his throat, threw the plane onto automatic pilot and turned toward Meg. "Marie's come back."

Meg caught her breath, but she didn't speak.

"She's at Milly's place in San Francisco. She wants to come back here."

When Meg was able to speak, she asked, "Do you want her to?"

"No! Definitely not. But, maybe I ought to talk to her. You know, finish this thing off. Maybe she does have her act together. Should I let her come?"

"Why ask me? What do you want to do? Are you afraid to see her again?"

"I don't know yet." The two gazed unseeing at the eye-level spectacle of Mt. Rainier, appearing pink in the misty sunlight. Neither spoke.

"Maybe you ought to consider what Amelia said. You aren't a young man anymore, and this is a long, energy-draining trip."

"Will you shut up and listen, just for once!"

Meg, surprised at his angry words, replied, "Sorry. I don't know what to say to you... or what you want me to say. I wish I knew the words to lift your pain, to give you some answers. I wish I could help you with this... situation."

"Why? You do know what to say, but why should you say anything like that?"

"Because I care, Hal. Because Marie is a ghost. She's always there, behind your words."

"I don't think I've mentioned her more than once or twice."

"You don't have to."

"Then you think I should see her and get rid of the ghost?"

"You're still married, aren't you? She's around you all the time, like your rooster. Always present. Do you want to get rid of her? Or do you want her back?"

"Damn you! You don't make anything easy, do you? I'd hoped you'd tell me… oh, forget it. Let's get back to earth…" He snapped back to manual controls and banked the plane around, adding under his breath, "in more ways than one."

"Not just yet. Here, let me take the controls." Without a word, he shifted the dual controls to Meg and sat back. She continued, "I don't think there is an easy way. No, I don't know the answers. But I'll bet you do."

Hal had closed his eyes. After a moment, he asked, "And what if he came back… Wilson, I mean? What if your husband waltzed in here and said, 'I'm back!' What would you do?"

Meg hadn't ever thought of that possibility. She had buried her husband, knew that Wil was gone forever. "I guess I'd take out the memory of him, dust it off, and look at it again. My life has changed since he died. I have changed in the time he's been gone. You've changed. I'm sure that Marie has changed too."

"All these years…"

"You may have to take out her memory and compare it to the real thing. Perhaps it's time to find out exactly how you still feel — hurt, angry, lonely. Can you deal with the real person, the real Marie?"

"Like maybe I have to stand toe to toe and tell her?

"Something like that. You have to listen too."

"Okay, I'll talk to her. But I think I'll wait a couple weeks."

"Come on, Hal. Let's go back and face your family. You and they can have a long talk. Get this thing out in the open. You know, it may make them feel better to know you'll be getting in touch with Marie. You might tell them that first."

"You're right. God, I hate it when you're right. But I'm still going to wait a couple weeks to go down there. Hey, Meg, once more around Mt. St. Helens before we head home? I'm feeling much better."

"Just one more thing. I'm going with you to Japan. And that's that! I never told anybody this, but I'm afraid of being left behind. I was the kid that got left behind at a gas station — only it was a church supper — and I still get a chill when I think of somebody leaving me behind. I don't intend to get left out of this one. Not one more word about it."

Hal almost cheered as he felt the weight of his orneriness lighten at last.

Meg banked the plane again and headed toward the mountain before turning back toward Harmony Field. She took the plane down for a smooth landing and taxied toward the hangar before she noticed Hal. He sat speechless… and smiling.

WHAT TO DO ABOUT MARIE

"WHAT A WAY TO CELEBRATE A BIRTHDAY." Hal tried to sound grumpy as he and Meg walked back to his apartment, his waiting children, and the delicate question of Marie. "What if they gang up on me? What if..."

"Stop! You'll what-if yourself to pieces before you start. Just walk in and gather your son and daughter together — I'll distract Melee and Toni — and put it to them straight out. 'Your mother wants to come back here.' Then shut up and listen."

"Sounds so easy when you say it. We'll see."

The two had reached the apartment; the rain had begun to fall again, harder this time. They hurried through the door, laughing when they tried to go through at the same time.

"Good flight?" Charles asked.

"Spectacular," Hal answered. "Yup! Spectacular." He cleared his throat. "Uh, Charles... and Amelia, would you step in the other room with me for a moment. Toni, maybe you could get Meg something to drink. Any wine left?"

"Sure, Hal. How about a glass for you?"

"Not right now, sweetheart. This won't take long."

Once inside Hal's room, the three stood awkwardly until Hal motioned for them to sit down... somewhere, anywhere. Amelia took the bed and Charles turned around the easy chair that had been facing the window. "What's up, Dad? Is this about Meg or...?"

"No. This is about your mother."

"Mother?" Charles' face fell serious and he shot a look at Amelia, who didn't seem surprised. "What about Mother?"

"Well…" began Hal, "she's come back. Turned up at Millie's restaurant and wants to come up here. What do you think?" He remembered Meg's instruction and planned to remain silent and listen.

"Wait a minute. You can't just spring this on us like that. Millie? You knew she was back and didn't say anything…"

"I couldn't, Chuck. I didn't know how."

Charles jumped out of his chair and paced, much like his father paced when confused. "Millie, where's she been? Why did she leave us? How does she look? Is she sick or…"

"Whoa! I'll answer all your questions, but the big one that Dad wants answered is whether you want her to come up here. She's staying with me for the time being. No, she isn't sick or anything. Apparently, she just misses her family. She…"

"What? Misses her family? After twenty years she suddenly remembers she has three children and a husband and… and a grandchild. Or does she know about Melee? Oh, I see. Too many questions." Charles stopped pacing and looked over at Hal, who sat fiddling with a thread on his sleeve. "Dad? What do you think? What do you want to do with her?"

Hal looked up, hoping Amelia would answer his son's questions, but she said nothing. "Let's see. The big question, do you want to see her… here… maybe have her come back and live… here?" The very idea caught him suddenly and he winced.

Charles closed his eyes and appeared to be considering. Actually, he was arguing with himself. Of course he wanted to reconnect with his mother; he wanted to see her, hold her close and remember the good times. He wanted to make sure she was… what? In good health? Not terminally ill? Not crazy? Or did he want to make his life go back to where it was this morning... spending time with his father, his wife and daughter, his sister? Did he want to go on without wondering where and how his mother was?

"Dad, I need to know. I need to know how she is, how she looks, where she's been, and why... why she left us in the first place. I need to know."

"Amelia? What are your thoughts?" Hal asked.

Hal's daughter had dreaded that question. She too was unsure of her feelings. Still, she had most of the answers Charles sought. She had seen Marie and knew... or sensed... that she was lonely, growing older, and somehow needed to settle some accounts in her life.

"I think you ought to invite her here... for a visit... to spend some time with her and make your peace, both of you. Wiley and I have..."

"Wiley? He knows she's back? Am I the last to find out?" Charles' eyes grew wide and he sputtered. "Nice family I have."

"Chucky, we were trying to protect you. I know how close you were with Mom. She's been staying at Wiley's place in Houston. She just came to San Francisco a couple weeks ago... and..."

"Ohmygod, this just gets better and better." Charles now appeared bereft, to the point of feeling abandoned by his family. Well, at least he'd have his mother back. "Okay, Toni and I can put her up at my place. It'll give her a chance to get acquainted with Melee. Yes, Dad, I would very much like to have my mother come here. How soon?"

"That's just it, son. I want to go to San Francisco and talk with her before bringing her here. She and I have some things to settle. I know... you are her children. But I'm still her husband.

And…" he grinned for the first time, "there are some grownups things we have to discuss."

"Want to fly back with me Sunday, Dad?" Amelia asked. "I'd love to have you."

"No, I can't just take off. For one thing, my Grasshoppers have a very important game coming up — season opener — and I've promised some training sessions. For another, Meg is almost ready to test-fly the plane and I…"

"I can do that, Dad. You know that I planned to take it up when it's ready."

"Sorry, Charles. This is my plane, my responsibility, and my expedition. I will test fly it."

"Okay, you two," Amelia cut in, "settle this between yourselves. I'm flying home Sunday and you're welcome to come along, Dad. If not, you can fly down and talk with Mom as soon as possible. She's anxious. I'm sure you can appreciate that."

Hal pouted again. "It's not like she's been waiting for twenty years or anything," he muttered. "Okay. I'll clear my runway and take off as soon as possible. I'll call you when I'm headed that way. Okay you two? Are we in agreement?"

Charles nodded sullenly, then suggested, "Let's not bother Melee with this yet. She'll have time later to think about her grandmother. And I'll talk to Toni as soon as we leave today."

"Group hug," Amelia announced as the three clung to each other, feeling the pain, the relief, the sadness, and the joy of the moment.

NOAH NEEDS CONVINCING

THE RAINY WEATHER CONTINUED and work on the plane moved ahead, almost on schedule. On a day when Meg was waiting for some parts to arrive, she decided it was time to catch up on her own business. She sat with Noah one afternoon in his office in the Webster Classics hangar.

Noah handed her some papers and observed, "You seem preoccupied today, Mom. Don't you want to see how many new orders we're getting since we moved up here? Three more since Christmas. Moving here was a good idea. Less competition, nice weather... at least until this rain set in. Isn't this supposed to be spring?"

"Sorry, I guess I *have* been preoccupied, worrying about Hal. He's supposed to leave soon to meet with Marie. I wonder if he'll bring her back with him. I wonder if he'll take her to Japan instead of... I just wonder..."

"Why Mother dear, you're more interested in that man than you're letting on. And what's this about Japan?"

"You must know why Hal wants this plane." Meg dodged the question.

"Yes, I've heard about his cockamamie scheme to fly it, but what's this about someone going with him? Not you, I hope."

"Oh nothing. Forget I said anything."

"Okay, but what about your interest in who flies with him? Are you... and Hal..." He left the question unfinished.

"Noah, of course not. He's a client and... almost a business partner. He lets us lease this space in return for my work on his plane. It's a business deal."

"Then why would you even consider going with him? You aren't telling me that he asked you to fly in that plane with him? Come on, Mother, talk to me."

"Well okay. Yes and no. I want to fly this trip with him, and he's been reluctant."

"Reluctant? Good for him! I'm a bit *more* reluctant. I'm putting my foot down. My mother is not going to fly in that plane, and certainly not across an ocean in an open cockpit with an old nut like that."

"Oh then it would be all right if I flew across alone? Or with another nut? Or in a closed cockpit?"

"You know what I mean."

"Just because Ellen is afraid to fly doesn't mean all women are."

"Leave my wife out of this. Ellen didn't grow up around planes. I did. I know they can kill you."

"Amelia Earhart didn't have any fear at all of planes like mine."

"And look what happened to her. She disappeared in the same ocean that your Hal is planning to cross. No, Mother, no!"

"I'm afraid it isn't up to you to decide, my pet. I'm old enough to make my own decisions. Sorry, but I want to go. And if Hal agrees… I think I have him pretty well convinced. Now, let me look at those new contracts. We're going to have to add a couple more mechanics, aren't we? And the Anderson family's pair of Wacos should be ready for testing before I leave. Can you handle that?"

"Mother, please. Business is not what I want to talk about. Let's settle this other thing before we talk about work."

"I thought we had settled it. Hal will be leaving the first week in June. That gives us just a little more than two months to install the rest of the interior of the plane and get the equipment in place."

"No, dammit, Mom! I'm talking to you as a son to his mother, not as a business assistant to the boss. It's you that I'm worried about. What if you… what if you… Mom, please reconsider."

"Noah, you're a grown man. We have to live separate lives. You have Ellen and your career. I have my career and now this trip." Meg stood up and moved around behind the desk to follow her words with a hug for her son. They stood together for a moment before Noah backed away.

"Right, Meg," he said, using his grownup tone of voice. "This won't be easy, but I'll try to understand."

"Let's just take it one step at a time. And the first step is you taking over here when I go to Japan in June. Can you handle that?"

"Looks like I'll have to."

Meg patted her son's arm before leaving the office and returning to the hangar where Hal's plane sat, awaiting finishing touches. She went over Noah's words as she opened the boxes that had just been delivered. The altimeter and some hardware. *He can't be that against me living my own life*, she thought.

She connected the altimeter before she continued to finish off the control panel, so immersed in the work she didn't hear Hal enter the hangar.

"How's the plane coming?" he called out.

Startled, Meg turned and recovered enough to answer with another question, "When are you going to San Francisco?"

"Right after I see this thing fly."

"Pack your bags. I've got the control panel in and the equipment installed."

"All of it? A radio?"

"Not yet. I'm still looking for the right one."

"Did the new gas lines get in?"

"Yep. They arrived Monday and we installed them yesterday. I'm using temporary gas tanks for now."

"Well, let's take 'er up."

"We're about to pump in some fuel to try out the tank structure. The plane will be ready for a test flight before we install them permanently. We're running some other checks today and maybe it'll be ready to fly by Friday. Charles said he'd…"

"Charles, my Aunt Prudence. I'm taking it up for the test. Are you crazy? Do you think I'd let anyone else fly my plane?"

"But he said…"

"Never mind what he said. I'm flying the test. Period."

"Okay, I'll meet you here Friday, eight a.m. Weather's on our side. The morning clouds seem to be burning off by mid-day."

DANCING WITH CLOUDS

FRIDAY MORNING DAWNED CLOUDY, but not raining, and Hal rushed through breakfast to meet Meg and his new plane. The bays of the hangar stood open and a brief break in the clouds let the sun peek through to shine on the new, bright yellow Vega that sat sunning like a golden animal in the new day's light. When Hal walked past the propeller, he patted it gently before he noticed the name on the side of the fuselage, printed in bold black letters: HARMONY'S HOPE. He moved to touch it, to feel the rough canvass with his fingertips. He caressed the wing gently, as a mother caresses a new-born.

"It's beautiful. Beautiful. It's just like... before." His voice broke. As tears welled up, he blinked them away and added, "like... before."

Meg watched him climb into the cockpit and strap on the cap she had remembered to order for him. He nodded at her and wordlessly tossed her a set of keys and pointed at his blue and white Cessna. She spun the propeller and stood back to watch him start the engine and fasten the canopy. He sat for a moment, enjoying the growling beat of the plane, the smell of fresh oil, and the feel of the craft responding to the new life just spanked into it.

Hal mouthed the words, "Good job!" and signaled a thumbs-up as he released the brakes and turned the nose toward the taxi lane and the end of the field.

Meg climbed into the Cessna 150 high-wing and started the engine, pulling the plane behind the yellow bird. She wished she'd had time to install the two-way on the radio so she could talk to him, hear how it handles. Feeling the distance between the two planes, she settled for a wave out the window.

At the end of the runway, Hal signaled back that he was ready to fly. He pressed one foot firmly on the brakes and gently pushed forward on the throttle, feeling the strain under his foot, testing the engine response. At full throttle he released the brakes, gently allowing the engine to do its thing, pulling the plane down the runway.

Smoothly, the yellow bird lifted off the ground and reached for the sky. Like a young golden eagle, it raced immediately for the air up near the clouds. The plane obviously handled well enough without its load, responding to the soft touch — a powerful engine and a light plane. *I can't wait to see how it handles when we're fully loaded for the trip.*

Meg's plane took off right behind Hal's Vega and found an observation site just below the yellow bird. There she watched his plane overhead, marveling at its strength and grace. *This is a champion, a winner, a star.*

Any white-winged seagull soaring through the blue morning sky that day would have been treated to a game of tag played by two graceful airplanes — one a sky-blue and white bird much like the gull and the other a canary yellow beauty that challenged the sun for attention.

Like a baseball hero basking in the limelight, the yellow bird seemed to be basking in its own beauty. Then it turned its nose upward and headed up through the clouds. Hal smiled as he spotted his Cessna. *I'll lose her. Betcha can't catch me!*

The yellow bird banked into the white mist and disappeared from Meg's view. Upstairs, above the clouds, alone, Hal turned to circle, keeping far enough away, then diving back into the clouds. He calculated correctly and easily moved into a spot on her blind side.

Through his side window, Hal sat, amused, watching as Meg searched for the bird. Then he raced past the gull, saluting briskly with one hand. Meg smiled, relieved, and waved back. He motioned her to follow, and the two planes headed back up through the clouds into the sunshine.

For the next few minutes, the morning sun was the only witness to a waltz in the blue clear skies above the white cotton-ball clouds. Meg rolled her plane and motioned Hal to try one. He followed, then added a loop, which Meg imitated. Hal pulled off a right wing dip, then a left, occasionally letting out a whooping yell. Ecstatic, she watched him somersault and dive; he watched her copy the wing dips before flying directly into the bright sun and disappearing.

Artfully, Meg spun around the yellow bird and popped up on Hal's right, just behind his line of vision. She glided up alongside and they flew together for a moment before going into another loop as one, choreographed only with hand signals between the pilots.

Both planes then pointed their noses straight ahead and took turns making wide outer circles, then rejoining the other. Hal brought his plane beneath hers and let her feel the reduced wind pressure, rather like an effortless glide. As her plane rested, she too rested, gazing around at the mountains that poked their heads through the low clouds.

Then they reversed positions and she flew beneath his plane, letting the yellow bird take a rest.

Vigor renewed, the pair resumed their chase until Hal noticed the gas gauge very close to Empty. He motioned a landing to Meg. They circled their cloud one more time, then dove into it. Breaking clear, they each took their bearings and headed for home.

Hal landed first, reluctantly but smoothly. Meg followed, taxiing up behind him to the hangar. She shut off the engine, feeling giddy from the high altitude waltz.

What happened up there? Did Hal feel it too? She climbed slowly out of his Cessna, not trusting her legs just yet. As she turned to jump down, she fell right into Hal's arms. He held her tightly; she didn't try to leave. They stood there, locked together, for a long time before he whispered, "Meg." He moved his head back to look at her before he kissed her, softly, passionately, on her lips. Then embarrassed, he hoarsely began, "We did it!" His voice returned and he repeated, "We did it! We built ourselves a plane that will fly around the world maybe. We did it!"

"Yes, Hal. We did it," Meg agreed quietly. Then he kissed her again. This time he noticed. He held her closely as his brain tried to process the feelings. He moved his hands to her shoulders and pulled back as he realized...

"When did this... happen?"

"Somewhere in a cloud deck, over there by the mountain, I think."

"Why didn't you tell me?"

"The two-way wasn't connected."

"Then we'd better connect it," he said simply.

The sun broke through the clouds just then to watch the waltz continue on the ground. "I knew you'd see the light," Meg whispered.

WHEN A GIRL NEEDS HER GRANDPARENTS

THE RAIN BECAME SERIOUS THE FOLLOWING DAY. On a rainy Saturday, Melee and Meg continued their work on the small model plane that was Hal's birthday present — a World War I Jenny. Hal sat reading as Doodle-do pecked at the carpet.

"Granddad, were you ever scared when you were flying? I mean during the war? Or when you were barnstorming with Grandma?"

"How do you know about barnstorming?" Hal asked.

"Mom told me. She said you and my grandma used to give rides to kids in your plane."

"You bet we did, kiddo. We used to weigh them on a little doctor's scale and charge them a penny a pound. Quite the gimmick to draw crowds. Once this guy who weighed over 300 pounds — 314 to be exact — paid his three dollars and fourteen cents and then couldn't climb into the plane. We pushed and prodded and pushed some more, but he couldn't make it."

"Mercy, what happened to him?" Meg asked.

"He just walked away. We tried to give him his money back, but he said no, it was worth it just to be that close to a real *aeroplane*."

"Did you do tricks too?" Melee looked up. "You know, acrobatics?"

"Ah that was the best part. Your grandma loved to fly along when I'd do the loops and rolls. She wanted to work up an act where she'd walk on the wing, but I put my foot down. She was always trying stunts like that." Hal leaned back for a moment, remembering. "Yeah, we had some real dandy planes then."

Meg glued a piece of the aileron and gently held it in place to dry. "Melee, I have replicas of all the planes your grandfather flew. Like this one. The one we're working on is just like the old Jennys that used to fly during World War I."

"You didn't tell me you were in that war, Granddad."

"I wasn't!" He glared at Meg. "Contrary to some opinions, I'm not that old."

"But these planes were very popular after the war too. In fact, they were some of the first planes flown in World War II."

"Granddad, were you in World War II?"

"Yup. Flew all over the Pacific." Then he added, speaking directly to Meg. "Just about everywhere... except Japan."

Meg pretended not to notice. "The early pilots, like your granddad, risked their lives to learn more about planes. Daredevils, barnstormers, NASA astronauts — they're the ones we remember. Yet, it was the people who ran the thousands of small airports all over the country that kept them going. It's just that nobody thinks about them much."

"Where'd you buy your planes back in the old timey days, Granddad?"

Hal smiled at his granddaughter. "There weren't airplane stores then, sweetie, we built our own. There were a couple of guys around here who designed some dandies. One was a lightweight plane that could fly for hours with just a few drops of fuel. Once he flew all the way to New York for something like twenty-seven dollars in fuel. Of course, fuel was cheaper then, but coast-to-coast for twenty-seven..."

"I've never heard that one, Hal. Who was he?"

"Can't remember his name now, but he sold a bunch of those planes. Didn't last, though. They were too lightweight and wouldn't hold still in heavy winds. Most of the early planes used for racing were lightweight and built for speed rather than distance."

"Sort of like the hang gliders we build now," Melee offered. "In all kinds of shapes and sizes to catch the wind, but not too strong."

"It's all the same principle. A little air under you and… you fly," Hal told her. "Kinda like those homeruns you'll be hitting soon. Which reminds me, are we going to get the same team again this year? My Grasshoppers need more practice before the first game, scheduled April 1, I think."

"Grand…dad!" Melee sang the word, stretching it out. "You know you can't get rid of this team. They'll all be back, except Erin. He moved away. And you should see Tanya. She's been swimming all winter on the school team and she's going to hit homers like a pro."

"I'll believe that when I see it. Meg, how about a fill-up on your soda?"

"Sure, Hal. Thanks."

"And speaking of fill-ups. Have the big gas tanks come yet? It's been a month since we contacted them."

"They arrived two days ago. We're working on them now. If we change to high octane fuel, we may be able to reduce the amount we need to carry."

"Gee, this is just like it must have been back then," Melee said.

"Back in the good old days of yore, you mean?"

"Yes... I guess... I wish I could go too."

"I'll bet you do. You'd probably want to walk there on the wings."

Melee missed the sarcasm and asked, "Granddad, may I run over to Tanya's for a while? We have to talk... you know, girl stuff... baseball and airplanes."

Hal and Meg laughed and Hal told his granddaughter, "Sure, go ahead. Tell Tanya hi, and tell her we practice next week. And take Doodle-do with you."

Melee jumped up, shooed the rooster ahead of her, and waved goodbye. Hal moved over to join Meg at the model-building table. "How are things with you?" He tried to sound casual.

"I'm okay. Noah has been hassling me to stay home and let you fly this by yourself, but I have some things to deal with too."

"Yeah, like what?"

"Like being afraid."

Hal looked up to see if she was kidding. She wasn't. "Afraid? Of getting lost... being left behind... being alone... or crash landing?"

"It's a combination of pushing away from Noah and... getting closer to you, losing him before I have you. I don't want to get left behind again, Hal."

"Why would that bother you now?"

Meg took a deep breath before she answered. "Marie... coming back."

"Marie?" Hal turned to face Meg.

"If Marie… well, I wish you'd resolve that soon."

"I've decided. I'll go down to California next week and talk to her. I don't want her back here. Do you understand? It's been too long." He took his time before he continued. "And you're going to Japan with me. Yup! You're going with me. I've decided. I'm the pilot, and what I say goes, and…"

But he got no further. Meg wanted to hug him, and had a difficult time keeping her hands on the model airplane. She broke in with, "Oh Hal, we'll have such fun. It's going to be hard, but if anyone can have fun, we will… you and I… we will. Thank you. Thank you."

"Meg, why is having fun so important to you? All I see you do is work, not have fun."

"My work is my fun. That's why I do it."

"But don't you do other things… for fun? How do you spend your time when you're not working?"

"Well, I… uh… I read. I watch television once in a while. I… that's about all. What? Should I take up golf or tennis or something? I haven't time. Why are you interested in my leisure activity?"

"I don't know. It just seems like you keep talking about having fun, making work fun. But you don't play games or go hiking or swim or ride a bicycle. Have you ever ridden a bike?"

"Hal, what is this about? Yes, I used to swim and ride bicycles and play… all sorts of things, but I'm a grownup who loves working on old planes. That is my fun."

The admiration showed in his eyes as Hal said, "Marguerite Webster, you are some kind of woman. A very special kind."

Meg could sit still no longer. Her hands escaped and she threw her arms around his neck before he could dodge them. The kiss she gave him was a grateful kiss, gentle, light as balsa wood, and very sincere.

Hal had his arms around her and didn't want to let go. He wanted to stay and he needed to back off. "Well... uh... now then... we've got *fun* work to do if we're going to take off on June 9."

Meg leaned back and asked, "Why is June 9 so important?"

"That's the same date as my first flight attempt. June 9, 1933."

"Then yes, we have work to do. The fuel changeover system has to operate without a hitch. Oh, by the way, some guy named Kevin from the FAA called for you at my office yesterday and left a message. The number is on my desk."

"FAA? Why would they call me there? I'll get the number and check with Charles at the office Monday."

"I must go. It's been... pleasant... spending the afternoon here. But I can't spend Saturdays loafing around."

Hal stood up and walked with Meg to the door. "Make sure the pilot's seat is soft and comfortable. Come on back for dinner tonight; I'm cooking."

Meg turned to go, then called back over her shoulder, "By the way, that was the nicest kiss you gave me..."

"I didn't...", but Meg was walking away with a backward wave.

WHAT DOES THE FAA WANT?

HAL WAS HOLDING THE TELEPHONE RECEIVER as Charles walked into his office Monday morning. He dialed a number before he asked, "Charles, did you take a call from some guy named Kevin from the FAA last week?"

"No, were you expecting one?"

"No, but Meg…" Hal signaled his son that someone had answered. "Hello, Kevin Waring please. This is Hal Harmony from Harmony Field returning his call. (pause) Okay, I can hold."

Hal put his hand over the mouthpiece and spoke to Charles. "Meg got a call at her office for me. Wonder what they want. The FAA hasn't been around here, have they? You haven't mentioned my venture, have you?"

He turned back to the phone. "Oh, hello, Kevin? This is Hal Harmony. What is it you want?" He listened for a few minutes, his face drooping slightly, then he threw back his head and laughed. "Whoever dreamed up a cockamamie story like that?… oh yeah, every few years some young reporter comes across the story and looks me up and writes about it. A young woman was in here a few months ago. The story just won't die… What? Somebody suggesting I ought to try the flight again? Unbelievable! Nonsense! What will they think of next to fill their papers? (long pause) The EAA? What would they want? No, Kevin, the FAA has nothing to worry about. Do you think I'd be foolish to try a trip like that? In this day and age of super planes and jets? At my age? Don't you worry about it, Kevin. If I decide to go, I'll let you know." He laughed again, hung up, then turned to glare at Chuck.

"Charles Augustus Harmony, how do you suppose the FAA got hold of a tale like that? They think I'd attempt to cross the ocean in a vintage airplane. Where'd they pick up an idea like that? Charles Augustus, did you tell on your father?"

"Dad, I only mentioned that Mrs. Webster is here building her planes. Well, I might have let slip something about retracing old flight patterns... but I didn't mention specifics."

"Hell, Chuck, they all know me up there. They wouldn't hesitate for a minute to believe I'd try a fool stunt like this again. Now I'll have to go undercover."

"Too late, Dad. I'm afraid a reporter was here while you were in Montana, talked with Mrs. Webster and has the whole story."

"Drat! Damn! Go fly a kite, Miss Agnes! Why in the hell... what were you thinking... oh, damn it, Chuck. You've just ruined everything. I've got to find out what Meg... Mrs. Webster... told them."

"You don't have to hide your feelings from me, Dad. I've known for a long time there's been something going on between you two. I haven't seen those moony eyes of yours for a long time. Way to go, Dad!"

Hal stood up and aimed at the door, hunching his shoulders as he walked away quickly. At Meg's office door, he paused to collect himself, squared his shoulders, and stalked in, announcing, "Meg, we've got trouble."

"Now what? Good morning, Hal. What's happened? One of your kids putting their foot down again?"

"Worse. The FAA is telling me I can't go. And they're bringing in the Experimental Aircraft Association."

"Oh no, Hal. How'd they hear about this? Never mind, I think I know, and that's not important now. What did they say?"

"That young squirt Kevin, probably doesn't even know who Charles Lindbergh was, may not even know we once built our own planes… anyway, he says he heard we were…" Hal mimicked the FAA agent's voice, "…planning a trans-Pacific flight using an old plane without a radio."

"And you told him…?"

"I told him the story was cockeyed. Who would believe such an idea?" Hal paused, then added, "I don't think he bought it. He's going to be sniffing around here trying to find out more." As Hal remembered the rest, he asked, "Did you talk to a reporter?"

"Yes. This guy came around last week. Maybe I told him too much about the trip. Mostly I reiterated that this plane is an exact replica of the plane you used back when… and I told him you just wanted it for old time's sake. I didn't mention Japan. But *he* thought it would be a great gimmick, you know, advertising for the airport and my business, if you tried to make the trip again. It was *his* idea, honest."

"Don't worry about it. Doesn't matter anyway. We might have to move up the date. Still a long way away. If the reporter suspects we're pushing for June 9… did he *know* the date?"

"Yes, I'm afraid he did. In fact, he even suggested taking off on the same date as before."

Hal paced in front of Meg's desk, thinking. "Well, if they're expecting us to take off on the ninth, we'll have to do that. But let's take off from Japan. Surely, the U.S. FAA, and certainly the

EAA wouldn't have anything to say about our taking a boat trip to Japan and flying back."

Meg brightened, then scowled. "My work schedule doesn't allow for that extra week for shipping. Unless…" She looked at her calendar. "Maybe I can do the finishing on the boat. I could be ready to put this plane aboard a ship by mid-May. Another week of final touches as we sail, and it would be ready to fly home on… June ninth. We'll give ourselves a few days window in Japan to allow for weather."

"It just might work." Hal stopped pacing and put his hand to his chin. "June ninth. June ninth. It might work. I can feel that plane taking off and soaring up through the Japanese clouds, catching the eastward jet stream and…" He turned to Meg. "I don't remember feeling this way before the other tries. Meg, I think we've got ourselves an adventure neither of us will forget."

"One more hurdle. We have to test this baby with a full load of something — not gasoline."

"I can manage that. My buddy over at the hardware store has barrels of stuff that weigh plenty. Or we can fill kegs with water… that's heavy. In a week or so?"

"Yes, we'll be ready. Now, about the radio…" Meg held her breath.

"Think you have me, huh? Well, I found a small transmitter and receiver that will do for contacting the flight towers. But let's both agree not to use it during the flight unless we are right up against it. Promise?"

"Promise. It's a deal, the least we can do for the FAA."

"Let's celebrate tonight. Toast the FAA and practice eating Japanese food."

"Sorry, if we're going to ship this thing in May, I'll be working overtime."

"Come on, Old Girl, let your people have some overtime. April is still a week or so away, which gives us a month before we sail. Take the evening off, with me, please. About time you had some fun."

"When you put it that way..."

APRIL FOOL!

HAL PITCHED IN DURING THE NEXT FEW DAYS, helping add some finishing touches to the interior and calling around to find 900 pounds of something harmless. He finally located nine 100-pound barrels, which were to be installed in the plane on Friday.

More important events were scheduled that Friday. The first game of the 1983 baseball season was to get underway. By mid-afternoon, school was out, and Hal headed across the field to the baseball diamond for a few practice throws with the early bird Grasshoppers before the big game. Opening day on April 1 had dawned with a sprinkling of rain showers. But by mid-afternoon, the rain had given way to part sunshine, and by the time the team finished batting practice, the sun brightened the mostly blue sky.

As "batter up" was called, Hal's team gathered for a group huggle. [*Huddles* are for football; *huggles* are for small fry baseball.]

Into the second inning, Hal sat on the bench with his Grasshoppers. Melee sat next to him, her bat tracing pictures in the sand as Doodle-do pecked at the bugs she stirred up. Tanya, sitting next to Melee, shyly leaned over and called to Hal, "Coach, will you let me bat this time? Please, Coach. Can I take my turn? I've been practicing since last year. Betcha I can hit one."

"Okay, Champ. Show me what you can do."

The hitter popped out with a fly ball and Tanya picked up a bat. She walked to the plate accompanied by the groans of her teammates. One brief scowl from Hal and they quieted down. The pitcher didn't waste any time. First one, a low ball. Tanya took a swing, missing it by a mile. She swung at the second pitch too, this time coming a tad closer, but still batting at air. On the third pitch, she glared at the pitcher, who tossed a neat throw right across the plate, in the strike zone. Tanya took a weak swat at it, but again, missed. She struck the bat on the ground, then slunk dejectedly back to the bench.

"Sorry, Coach. I guess I was too excited. But next time… give me another shot at bat. Next time, I won't be so scared."

"Sure, Tanya. Don't think about it. I know how you feel. You'll get another chance at bat… next inning."

Melee had avoided watching Tanya strike out by looking backward at the cheering grandstand. While it wasn't very *grand*, the set of bleachers accommodated a few proud parents and a few classmates.

"Granddad, there's a lady over there watching you. I never saw her before. Do you know her?"

Hal turned to look, blinked, shut his eyes tight, then blinked again. The woman, a washed-out blond in her late sixties, stood out clearly. Overdressed for baseball in a hot pink pantsuit and strappy heels, she appeared to smile at him, her prettiest.

"What the…" Hal sputtered. "Is this some kind of April Fool joke? Marie?" Melee watched as he stood up slowly and walked toward her.

"Hi Hal," Marie chirped. "Long time. You look… older."

"I am older," Hal stammered. "About twenty years older. Where you been? What are you doing here?"

Marie, aware that many eyes were watching her, whispered to Hal, "Could we talk without entertaining your team?"

Hal turned around to see the entire team of Grasshoppers staring. "Go on with the game. Go on," he called. "Whoever's up next… hey, Jake, can you coach both teams?" Obviously befuddled, surprised, and confused, Hal took Marie's arm and led her away. "Come on, Marie, let's walk over to my place. Charles fixed up an apartment for me, and I live right here on the field. Still. Been here all this time. But you… I'm babbling. You're back. You're here. Have you seen Charles?"

"Steady, old buddy. I know you're surprised. Surely you knew I'd come back. Yes, I went to the office but Chucky wasn't there. They told me where you were. It's good to see you, Hal. I've missed you."

"Sure. Sure. You never came to see me for twenty years; couldn't have missed me too much. So why you here now?"

"There'll be time to talk. Let me catch my breath. I'm a little… uh, startled too. Seeing you… older… but still with that look in your eye… it's a bit overwhelming. You do look good, Hal."

Both out of words for the moment, they walked silently for a time. About halfway across the field, Marie stopped and reached for Hal's hand. "I want to come back," she began. "I want to get to know my children, play grandmother. Maybe it's because I'm getting on, but I feel like I've missed a part of my life. I think it might be you and the kids." She paused a moment before asking, "You're not married or anything, are you?"

Hal slowly pulled his hand back and resumed walking, keeping slightly ahead of her. "If you recall, Marie, I am married — to you. Although I probably could get a divorce, very easily, I never did. You deserted me... the family... you walked away from all of us."

Marie started to say something, but Hal continued. "Why now? Why have you come back now? What do you want?"

"Sounds as if you were waiting for me. You knew I'd come back." Marie ran a few steps to catch up and walk beside Hal.

"Maybe. Amelia told me you'd talked with her. But hell, Marie, it's been twenty years. The kids have grown up without you, I've..."

"You never tried to find me? The plane was registered. It wouldn't have been that difficult to find me."

"What I knew was that if you had crashed the plane, I'd have been notified. Guess I knew you were a good pilot, so I wasn't worried. I knew you were unhappy, I just hoped..."

Marie lowered her voice as she said, "I sold the plane. Didn't want you to find me."

"Well, where in the blue blazes have you been? The kids have had an awful time with your leaving. They were devastated... and it shows in their lives. Amelia can't stand being married, won't have kids. Wiley..." Hal raised his voice, along with his anger and his blood pressure. "Wiley can't find anyone to meet his high standards for a wife... a woman who wouldn't leave him. And Charles? Charles has turned off his feelings altogether. You have screwed up this family righteously, Marie.

And now you waltz back in here and want to take up where you left off. Are you nuts?"

"Please, Hal. Calm down."

"I will not calm down. I'm mad, hopping mad, madder than I've ever been. You flew off and left me with three kids — that kind of mad."

"They were all grown up."

"Maybe in years, but they were your kids. And you left them. Never mind how old they were. They missed you too."

Marie caught the last word. "Ah, so you *did* miss me."

"Of course I missed you. I loved you... once. I loved you and needed you, and you walked out... no, you flew out. Things have happened, to both of us. We've both changed. And now you... you..." Hal took a deep breath. "Marie, I think it's time we use the word *divorce*. It's probably what you want; it's certainly what I want. We can still be in contact. You and the children can make your own arrangements; they're all grown up now. But you and I... it's over. You must see that."

"Yes, I know. I just thought... well, maybe it's for the best. Do you want to file whatever it is you have to file? I'll sign papers and it'll be legal." Marie closed her eyes for a moment before she said, "Maybe that's why I came here after all. To tie up loose ends."

"Marie, are you sick or something? You sound despondent."

"No, I'm healthy as a horse. I just didn't realize I needed to bring our marriage to a close. And if you need a reason, just tell them I deserted you. Desertion, that's a reason."

Hal was feeling light again. "Thank you, Marie. Yes, I'll file... and I don't need a reason. This is a no-fault state." He couldn't go on. They had reached the apartment. He absently opened the door and went inside. Marie followed.

Hal headed to the kitchen to get a glass of water. Marie looked around and spotted photographs. When she found one she didn't recognize, she said, "She was at the baseball game. One of ours?"

"You don't even know your own granddaughter. That's Melee... Amelia... Charles' daughter. She's eleven."

"And you didn't tell her I was her grandmother?"

"I'm not sure I want her to know. It's hard on kids to find and lose people they should be close to. Marie, what are we going to do? What do you want?" Hal drew a second glass of water, tossed in a couple of ice cubes, and went back into the living room.

Marie took the glass and sat down. "I thought I wanted to come back. But you don't seem all that pleased to see me. Maybe I ought to just get out of here and forget all about this place." She took a sip of water and paused for a long time before quietly adding, "I want to fly to Japan with you."

"What?" Hal's mouth fell open and he nearly dropped his glass. "Where in blue blazes did you hear about that?"

"There was a small item in the aviation newsletter. Said you were going to finish the flight you started back when. Are you?"

"Well, yes, but..."

"I thought I'd like to go with you. Be your navigator."

"No way! No, Marie..." That was when Hal remembered Meg. "No, I... er... I have... a... navigator."

"Chucky? Is he going with you?"

"No, not Charles. It's nobody you know. Now, I think you'd better turn right around before you cause more trouble. Go back to wherever you came from… where did you come from anyway?"

"Promise you won't get mad?"

"Marie, just tell me."

"I'm at Amelia's. Didn't she tell you that?"

"I mean before you went to San Francisco. Where have you been hiding?"

The woman took another sip of water, keeping her eyes away from Hal, and almost whispered, "I'm staying with Wiley in Houston. He's…"

"Wiley? My son Wiley?"

"Yes. Just the last year or so. When you didn't come back with Amelia last week, I realized you probably wouldn't ever come for me. So I came up here before going back to Houston."

"I had no reason, Marie. We have separate lives now. Can't you see that?" Hal's disbelief was returning to the angry spot. He spoke slowly, "Wiley. You're staying with my son and he never said a word. You're really something, kiddo."

Marie slammed her glass on the coffee table and stood up. "All right then, I'll get out of here. I'll catch a flight for Houston tonight. Where's your phone?"

"Good. That sounds fine… just fine with me. No, that's not fine. That's not fine at all. If you go back, then nothing's changed. And I think it's time we face what we have to do, now."

"I'm not sure what you mean."

"I've learned a hell of a lot lately about carrying baggage. I've carried the baggage of my aborted flight for fifty years and it's been damn heavy. And I've carried your baggage for twenty years. I think it's about time I lighten the load."

"What do you mean, Hal? You can send the papers to me."

"Not the divorce. What about them?" he asked, pointing to the pictures of their children.

"Yes, what about them? I haven't seen all my children together in years. And I haven't ever seen my grandchild, close up. Can't we sit down and work out some sensible arrangement so we can at least be friends...?" Hal almost choked as he set down his water glass and stood up to face his wife. Marie finished weakly, "Can't we stay in touch, kind of like a friend of the family?"

"For god's sake, Marie. You live with one son, fly in and out of Amelia's place. All you're missing is Charles and his family. Now you show up here and want to be a friend of the family? Lordy, you're their mother!"

The two stood face to face, each shouldering their own concerns, each trying not to remember. That was when their oldest child, Charles, walked in, breathless. "Mom? Mom? Is it really you?"

"Chucky," Marie cried out, reaching toward him. The young man ran across the room to hug her and they clung to each other in an attempt to reclaim twenty years.

When Charles lifted his head, he asked, "Where did you come from? How'd you get here? Why..."

"Your father and I are talking. Here, sit down next to me."

At that moment, Melee rushed into the apartment, a frightened look on her face. "We were winning, Granddad, but I got worried when I saw Dad run across the field. Is something wrong, Daddy?"

Charles reached out to his daughter. "No, Amelia. Nothing's wrong. There is someone I couldn't wait to see. Come here, meet… your… grandmother."

That was when Melee saw the blondish woman standing almost behind her dad. She shyly walked over and said the only thing she could think of, "How do you do."

"Not even a hug?" Marie countered. "Come here, dear. I haven't seen you since you were a tiny baby… at least a picture of you. Your Aunt Amelia keeps your baby picture at her house."

Marie gave Melee a slight hug and continued to hold her, as Charles asked, "Mom, how long are you here for? Will you stay… with Dad, or…"

Hal found his voice. "We were discussing that, Charles, when you arrived. Will you come with me while Marie gets to know her granddaughter?" He motioned to his son, and the two headed for the kitchen, leaving Marie and Amelia looking at each other.

When they were out of hearing range, Charles said, "Dad, I don't want to talk to you. I want to talk with my mother."

"Well, first you've got to talk to me. There are a few things you should know."

"Like what? What in blazes is going on here?"

"Marie is here because she wants to *reconnect* with the family. Suddenly. After twenty years of silence. She decides to reconnect with the family. Us, that is. She's already reconnected with Wiley and Amelia."

"What do you mean?"

"She's been staying with Wiley and she's dropped in on Amelia before. It seems we're the only ones she's stayed away from. And those two conspired with her to do just that. Now she wants to come back and *drop in* on us."

"Oh Dad, you must have this wrong. Mom wouldn't stay away from just us. She'd… she…" That was when Charles realized his mother probably had not come to see him. She hadn't cared enough for her oldest son in the past to get in touch with him; why now?

"Sorry, Charles. I don't want her back here. I'm not sure you do either. I've already told her how I feel. It's your turn now to let her know how you feel."

Talk about putting children in the middle between parental in-fighting. Charles' mother, who left him twenty years earlier, had just walked back into his life. Charles' father suggested he tell her to buzz off. The only reason seems to be that Charles' father didn't believe that Charles' mother cared about them. *Well then, Chucky*, the young man tells himself, *maybe you don't need her either.*

"Okay, Dad. I'll talk to her. Stay with Melee and we'll go for a walk."

Somehow, Hal sensed his son's turmoil. "Attaboy, Charles. I know how hard this is for you and, maybe Melee, but let's get it over with. I'm through putting things off and expecting them to go away." That was the first time Charles Harmony realized his father considered him a grownup.

When the two men returned to the living room, they saw Marie staring at Melee as the child showed her grandmother the half-finished model airplane. "What a daughter you have, Chucky. She's amazing, a real gem."

"Mother, will you take a walk with me? Melee, stay here with Granddad."

"Ooh, that sounds ominous, Chucky. Okay, let's walk."

Hal broke in. "Melee, maybe you can catch the end of the game if you hurry back now."

"Okay, but I..."

"If you hurry."

"Goodbye, Gran... Marie."

Marie turned back to Melee and called out, "See you later, alligator." Melee wasn't sure how to respond. She took off in the opposite direction, back to finish the season opening ballgame.

Mother and son walked slowly along the runway, each transported deep into the days when Chucky was growing up with a mother who ran the field café and a father who worked on airplanes over in the hangar.

"Mom, are you here to stay?" Before she could answer, he added, "Why did you come back... now?"

"Well, uh, your father and I have decided on a friendly divorce. I'll go back to Houston and back to work."

"And what about us — Melee and me?"

"You can come see me anytime. I'll come see you when I can. When Wiley flies into San Francisco, I sometimes go with him to visit Amelia. We all can spend some time together. I want to get to know all my grownup children... and my granddaughter..." She added a pensive "...the only grandchild I have."

"Mom..."

But Marie wasn't finished. She needed to unload; she wanted her son to understand. "Chucky, love, I was unhappy. Your father and I probably should never have married. We should have had a carefree fling and parted friends. He wanted to raise chickens and kids and fly airplanes. I wanted to see the world, play games, and make believe."

"But Mom, you... what took you away from me... us?"

Marie dreaded that question. How should she answer? "You may not understand this, but I knew your father would teach you all you needed to get on in the world. I'd have taught you to shoot for the moon, take chances, live for today, fritter your life away... as I've done. I ran away. Ran away not only from you, but from me. The problem is that everywhere I stopped, there I was."

"Mom..." Charles struggled to understand what she was saying. On one level he knew she had been unhappy as a young mother, but on another level — his level — he was unhappy without her.

"I have to finish. What have I been doing? Having fun while I grew old. I moved around, taking jobs that looked like fun, working in casinos, bars, bingo halls, swim clubs. I coached tennis and golf. In other words, I've played at living, trying to avoid the obvious. I moved around as the whim struck me. But mostly I've stayed in this part of the world, knowing that you, my children, were here."

The two had reached the end of the runway. There seemed to be nowhere else to go.

"Now I'm tired of playing games," Marie said, turning to face her son. "When I found Wiley, I decided to try playing Mother again. It was probably too late. I guess it's too late with you too."

"Yes, Mom. I guess it's too late for me too. When I first saw you, I wanted to believe you had come back for me, that we could take up where you left us. But I can see we've both got our own lives. We really don't share much anymore. Still..."

"I'll always love you, Chucky baby, you must know that. My love won't change. I've always loved you. I just couldn't..." Marie began to cry, softly reaching for her son.

"It's okay, Mom. It's okay."

"No it isn't!" Marie pulled back for a moment, then hugged Charles again. "But we can't fix it anymore."

MEG WEBSTER HAD SPENT THE DAY IN SEATTLE, looking for some last minute chrome fittings for Harmony's Hope. She had just poured herself a glass of wine and settled down at her desk to read the mail when the phone rang.

"Meg Webster," she said.

"Hello, Meg. It's me. Don't say anything, just listen. Marie is here."

"Marie? Your wife? She's at the field?" Of all the things Meg didn't want to hear, she had just heard.

"You got it. She came because she said she wanted to fly to Japan with me."

Meg was confused for only a moment, before she saw the desk calendar turned to April 1. She burst out laughing. "Oh Hal, you're really funny. I get it. April Fool! Come on now, you didn't think I'd fall for that, did you?"

"No, wait, Meg." Hal hadn't expected that response. "Wait! I'm serious. Dead serious." He lowered his voice. "Marie is here. I thought it was her April Fool joke too, but she's here and we talked. She's spending the night with Charles and his family, then she'll leave... she says she'll leave tomorrow." Dead silence on the phone line. "Meg? You there?"

"You're serious? Really?"

"Afraid so. I called to say I won't be over to the shop until late morning. I said I'd take Marie to Sea-Tac."

"Okay. We can talk tomorrow. Are you sure you're not kidding?"

"Oh yeah! Nothing for you to worry about. She may have come with other ideas, but I told her I had different plans. Meg, she's no longer a part of my life. That ghost you talked about is gone. Gone. Now, get a good night's sleep. Goodnight, Meg."

"Thanks for telling me. I'll see you tomorrow, when you get back. Good night." Meg replaced the phone receiver and took a long swallow of wine. She sat at the desk for a long time, trying to keep her mind from carrying her away. *How dare she? She's still his wife. What is her real reason for showing up? Not a trip to Japan. How'd she know about the flight anyway? Must be some action in the heavens,* she conceded. *Literally!*

DO YOU BELIEVE IN MIRACLES?

THE NEXT AFTERNOON MEG PUTTERED ABOUT, waiting for Hal. When he finally walked in, his face didn't show his feelings, nor did his choice of words, other than, "She's gone." Meg didn't ask for more.

Within a couple of hours, they had gone over placement of the fuel containers and were playing with the wires and switches when Melee ran into the hangar. She was wearing her baseball uniform and her face was flushed with excitement.

"Granddad. Tanya did it! We won the game. Tanya hit a two-base hit and drove in a run. Granddad, we won! And Tanya did it."

"Jumping grasshoppers! I forgot about the game."

"Tanya… won the game." Melee threw her arms around her grandfather and slumped against his chest.

"Take a deep breath, darlin', and then you can tell me. Did you ever doubt Tanya? All it takes is a chance. Hey, that makes our first win of the year. Way to go, pal. Good start."

Melee backed off to look up at Hal seriously. "It's only our second game, Granddad."

"But it's a good start. Better times are a coming."

Melee shuffled her feet and looked at the floor as she said, "I was the run she drove in. We won six to five. We won! We won!"

"Congratulations, pal-ee. So *you* were the winning run. Nice goin'. Just wish I'd have seen it."

"Nice going, Melee," Meg added. "You're getting to be a good player."

Melee's breath was almost back to normal when she spotted the plane. The last time she'd seen it, the parts lay about the hangar like the balsa wood parts of the model Jenny. "Is this it, Granddad? Is this the plane you're flying to Japan?"

"A beauty, huh?" He ran his hands over the yellow covering. "By the way, I haven't seen you since…. How'd you get on with your grandma?"

Melee giggled. "She wanted me to call her Marie. She wasn't too hot on me calling her 'grandma' and she wasn't too hot on me playing baseball. Said it was a boys' game. I told her we were Grasshoppers and they can be either boys or girls."

"Good shot."

Melee joined her grandfather in running her hand across the skin of the plane. "So this thing really flies. It looks just like your model, Meg. Only bigger."

"Yes, it really flies. We'll give you a ride in it when we get back," Meg promised.

Hal's head shot up. "Gee whiz, I never thought about when we get back. What'll we do with it? Put it in the Smithsonian, or the Flight Museum? Or…"

"We'll put it on display here and take people for rides. It… and you, Hal, will be famous, and people will come from miles around to see the plane and Harmony Field."

"Hold on there, dreamer. Ten minutes after we're home, the trip will be forgotten. Fifty years ago, we'd have been heroes. But this old world is too fast for this old plane."

"Maybe slowing down is what this old world needs, and maybe this plane will remind folks of that."

Tanya's game winning run wasn't the only near-miracle that day. Melee looked up at the hangar girders and called out, "Granddad… Granddad. Look! Look who's up on the rafter."

"What the... well, I'll be. Meg, look. Doodle-do has flown up to that girder. Roosters can fly. Can you beat that!"

"Looks like a good omen to me. If roosters can fly, so can this bird," she proclaimed, patting the yellow canary.

"Hi Hal," called Noah as he entered the hangar. He was dressed casually, but his expression remained all business.

"What are you doing here, son? It's Sunday."

"I need you to sign these, Meg. What're you looking at?"

Melee squealed, "Doodle-do. There, up on the rafter."

"So he is. I didn't know that roosters could fly."

"Neither did he! Come on, Melee," Hal said. "Let's go over to the office and tell your dad about this two-miracle day."

"Yeah, Tanya hits me home and Doodle-do flies."

Meg held up her hand. "Hal, before you leave, can I have a word?... in my office." Noah signaled that he was returning to his office, and left.

Melee couldn't wait. With a wave, she ran off to tell her father about the game, and about Doodle-do.

Doodle-do, high on his rafter perch, let out a loud proud rooster crow, "Cockadoodle-doo!"

Meg followed Hal into the office, closing the door behind her. Her face wore an expression of conspiracy. She lowered her voice and said, "Noah's been making male noises again, Hal, telling me he doesn't want me to fly to Japan."

"Hell, I thought he was over that. Well, just tell him you won't. Promise him you won't fly to Japan."

"But Hal, you said I could go."

"Listen to the words. *You* won't fly to Japan."

"Oh, he'll see through that. He knows you'll do the flying."

"Okay then, *promise* him you won't fly with me to Japan." Hal grinned at his own cunning.

Meg thought a moment, considering the words, before she heard Hal laugh. "I didn't say you won't sail with me to Japan and fly back!"

"You scared me there for a minute. But Noah doesn't fool easily. I'll have to face him, duke it out, so to speak. I'll put it on a business basis and maybe he'll understand." She thought for a moment before she said, "I've got it. I'll talk to him from a ship-to-shore phone after we've sailed."

"Coward."

"Oh yes. There's more to Noah than he lets on. I'm not even sure he understands how dependent he is on me... no, I don't mean for his finances, I mean... you know... emotionally."

"Not sure what that means."

"I'm his only parent. We work closely together. If something were to happen to me..."

"Come on, Meg. You know that..."

"Yes, I know. But he doesn't. Hear me out."

"If something were to happen to me, he'd not only lose his mother, he'd lose his job and possibly the life he knows. I'm not sure he's as close to Ellen as he is to me. I don't encourage it, but let's face it. He and I have been holding each other up for years. This won't be easy."

"Sounds to me as if it might be time to teach your boy to fly. If Doodle-do can do it…"

"All right, you win. I'll take him to lunch. It's always better talking to him in a crowded place."

"Attagirl, Meg!"

"Just one more thing — to settle Noah's mind. We'll have two cabins aboard ship, won't we?"

"Well now, do you think that's necessary?"

"Hal, you know you're still married. It wouldn't seem right…"

"Oh yeah, I forgot to tell you. Marie has agreed to sign a no-contest divorce decree. I'll be a free man. A single grandpa, if you will."

"But…"

"Okay, we'll have connecting cabins. How's that? I can say it now — legally — I like you, Meg Webster. I really… like you." Hal turned and left hurriedly before Meg could respond.

Meg sat at the desk for several minutes, tapping her fingers on the corner. She felt the same about Hal, and understood his reluctance to use the other l-word. It had been a long time since either one of them used the word the way they wanted to use it now.

Meg's mind slipped from "I love Hal" to "I love Noah", remembering the years when her son was a boy, how he followed her around the house, how he balked at going to school, how he hurried home to be near her as he did his homework. With a jolt, she looked again at his reaction when he was faced with going away to college. She recalled how he teased her to go back to school, finish her degree — with him.

Of course. No wonder this is a problem now. I've let it grow into one. Face it, Marguerite, you have needed him as much as he has needed you. Perhaps the time has come to learn to fly solo, and to help Noah do the same.

Having convinced herself that she was doing the right thing, she stood up and walked over to Noah's office, squaring her shoulders to look as businesslike as possible. She'd approach him as his business partner, then shift into her mother role.

"Noah, we're going to have this thing ready to go in about four weeks," she began. "Can you make sure we get that last shipment of panel hardware for the Anderson job on time?"

Noah appeared inattentive, pouring over some accounting books. "Sure," he muttered. "No problem. The Andersons will be flying before Memorial Day."

"Good, because I'll be leaving before Memorial Day."

Noah's head shot up. "Where are you going?" he asked.

"Let's discuss my itinerary over lunch. I'll buy. Are you almost finished here?"

"Mom..."

"Meg, please. And we'll discuss everything over lunch."

"Drive-up hamburgers?"

"No, sit-down deli. I'll wash up and be ready to go in about fifteen minutes. You drive?"

The noon crowd was disappearing from the deli as Meg and Noah placed their order at the counter and made their way towards a corner table.

"Now what's this itinerary you're so anxious about?" Noah asked as they settled down.

Meg took a long breath and tried to sound officious. "I'll be leaving in mid-May to sail to Japan and..." she lowered her voice, "...fly back with Hal. We plan to..."

"Wait a minute. You're not... you said... I thought you had decided... what the heck, Mom, I thought we settled this. You can't possibly be serious about flying in that plane across the Pacific Ocean. I don't care which way you go."

"Lower your voice," she whispered. "Of course I'm serious. And I'm going. That's that. Now, I'll need your support while I'm gone. You'll have to hold down things here, deliver the Wacos, schedule the work on the new blue Ryan, and..."

At that moment the waiter brought their food — soup and salad for Meg, a hamburger and potato slices for Noah. Meg took the opportunity to let her son cool off as she chatted with the waiter. "Perhaps you could bring us each a cream soda. Cherry all right with you, Noah?" She didn't wait for an answer, just nodded at the waiter. "Two cherry cream sodas."

By the time the waiter had left, Noah was seething. "Mother..." he snarled.

"Meg. Remember?"

"All right, dammit, Meg! I don't want you to go out there and risk your life for a lark."

"A canary," Meg offered, stifling a smile.

"This is not funny. Be serious. Don't go."

"I'm sorry, son. I'm so sorry for expecting you to understand this. I've overlooked your feelings and I apologize." She was shifting into mother-mode.

Noah took a large bite of hamburger; Meg sipped her soup, each involved with sorting out their own thoughts. After a few minutes, Noah spoke. "Okay, Meg, I think I know what's going on. I realize we've become much too close and I need to get my act together and carry on by myself. We've had this talk before, in a way. I get it."

"You're right. Whether or not I fly across the Pacific, Noah, east to west or the other way, I'll be out of your life one day. We should have faced this long ago."

"You'll never be out of my life. Like it or not, we're a team and have been for too long not to feel some loss without the other."

"You're right again, my dear. Perhaps I should have tried to make you more independent earlier, like when you found Ellen, but perhaps I needed you as much as you needed me. Well, son, the time has come to dissolve this partnership, and…"

"Dissolve? Are you firing me?"

"No, your job is not in danger. I'm talking about our relationship. It's time we dissolved…"

"Are you revoking my status as son?"

Meg took a deep breath. This was not going well. "Okay, say develop… in another way, in other areas. How about it? I'll try if you will."

"This won't be easy, Mom. It may take time. Do we have to do it all at once?"

"Let's try it a step at a time. And the first step is you taking over here while I go to Japan. Can you handle that?"

"Looks like I'll have to."

"Not 'have to'. This is an opportunity. I love you, and always will. You are my family… you and Ellen. It's not as if we're denying one another. It can be as if we're including others into our family circle." She reached across the table and patted her son's hand. "I want you to live a full life, with or without me. And this is the chance to get started — for both of us."

"And Hal?"

"You can depend on Hal to take care of... both of us. He's a fine pilot, a safe pilot, and..." She could go no further with Noah, not just yet.

"And you're a damn good navigator. You build sound planes and I should know better than to doubt your judgment. You always know what you're doing. It's just that..." Noah reluctantly made an attempt to take that thought ahead. "Of course I have misgivings about some man carrying off my mother. What about... ?" but he stopped there.

The mother-son-partners lunch ended with chocolate brownies.

CRUISING TO JAPAN

THE NEXT WEEKS FLEW BY, with Meg and Hal dodging FAA representatives who kept responding to rumors of a wild flight to Japan in an ancient plane. With each visit, Meg covered the name on the yellow bird and passed her work off as another custom-made replica.

Hal managed to be away from the field during those visits. Once, when an agent caught up with him, he solemnly swore that he had no plans to fly to Japan. Besides, he explained how his old plane probably couldn't make it half-way to the Aleutians.

Marie returned signed divorce papers in the mail and Hal filed them under Finished Business.

Tanya's baseball accomplishments increased to five more base hits and couple of two-baggers. She had moved up in batting order and shifted to a place of honor on the bench. Melee cracked out two home runs, and the Grasshoppers were looking good for the season. Summer was beginning to show its face in the Northwest and school would be over in three weeks.

One morning, Meg called to Hal as he returned from his morning flight.

"What's up, Mrs. Webster?" he asked as he entered the hangar and found her sitting in the cockpit of Harmony's Hope.

She leaned out to tell him, "We've installed the weight in the plane. It's full of... heavy stuff. Care to try it out now?"

"Do I? Can't wait. Let me get my goggles and hat." Meg smiled as she watched Hal scurry about, remembering what it felt like to be twenty and testing a new plane.

"Come on, sport. Time's a wasting. Let's take it up."

"Oh, not you too," Hal moaned.

"No other way. Remember, you'll have all of my... er... hundred-plus pounds to add to the weight. Let's do this together."

The team rolled Harmony's Hope out onto the runway, straining at the heavier load. The pilots securely strapped themselves in (another concession to Meg's concern for safety) without speaking. At last they started the engine and taxied laboriously to the end of the runway.

No one is sure whether or not they both held their breath through the entire takeoff, but it seemed that way when the plane became airborne and the pilot and navigator heaved sighs of relief. "It flies!" Hal mouthed the words. Meg returned a thumbs-up.

Throughout the testing, Meg made notes and Hal continued to smile. They passed low over the airport so the team could look at the underside of the plane in flight; they gauged the maneuverability of the vertical tail surfaces, and the ease of handling the rudder. Both deemed the plane worthy of a long flight.

The landing proved even handier than Hal had expected.

Nearing mid-May, Meg and Hal stood before the plane one warm evening and went over their plans again. They had booked a Japanese freighter to ship the plane. "I think I've found the right one," Meg had called out from the office a few days earlier. "An old friend tells me the crew will cooperate with us."

"Everything seems in place. It all should go well, partner," Hal told her.

"I've been over the check-list several times. Everything is done that can be. The rest will take place aboard ship. We're on our way."

"Sleep tight tonight. Tomorrow is a big day."

"Goodnight, Hal. Wheels up tomorrow."

As it played out the next evening, the plane was being loaded aboard the freighter when an FAA car drove up. One of the ship's crew, dressed in official looking orange overalls, fulfilled their promise to Meg and Hal, and motioned for the car to head toward another dock. When reporters showed up, they too were waved off by the Japanese team.

Only Noah and Charles accompanied their parents to the ship for farewells at the night sailing. "We'll finish servicing the plane during the trip across," Meg reminded her son.

Oh yes, one other thing. The freighter had only one available cabin for their travelers. Meg smiled and Hal gave her a hug as they waved goodbye to Seattle.

The trip turned out to be fun for the entire crew. They enjoyed watching their passengers as the two added finishing touches to the plane, clowning, making faces, and laughing as they worked.

In the evenings, the pair watched the sunset from the aft deck, arms around each other. Their meals were prepared below deck and enjoyed in the open air above. One evening just two days off the Japan coast, they had just completed a dinner of Japanese delicacies and were lounging on deck, bundled up against the cooler evening breeze.

"When we get to Tokyo, we can check out those three airports that Noah found for us," Meg said lazily. "We'll have to decide which one we can use without too much fuss. Did you check the weather today?"

"Yes. Everything looks fine. Ah, spring in Tokyo. That will be a treat. Ever been there?"

"No, I don't travel much. My husband said he traveled all he wanted to during the war. On leave, he liked the comfort and convenience of home. You? Travel much?"

"Only during the war; that was enough. Flew lots of local flights. I filed flight plans for one of Earhart's races once and ended up in St. Louis. Was glad to get back home."

"You grew up in Washington, didn't you? I really don't know much about you, Hal. Things like what kind of kid you were, that sort of stuff."

"I grew up on my dad's farm, where the airfield is now. He raised dairy cows for a while, but found chickens a better profit. Cows eat much more than chickens. As I got older and airplanes came on the scene after the war, the first one, Dad had a field lying fallow and let a couple of local flyers use it to land. They offered rides on weekends and split profits with Dad. Guess that's how I came to love airplanes so much. How about you?"

"I was closer to the Depression kids. We moved to California from Michigan, just ahead of the dust bowl refugees. The whole place was going through a kind of addiction to talkies when I learned about movies. I loved going to the pictures, especially after they added sound. Funny, I used to wonder why we couldn't have moving picture shows in our homes. And now we have television."

"We had a set kinda early, black and white of course, but on the farm the reception was loud and clear; we built an antenna on the windmill. Michigan, huh? You should be making model automobiles." They both laughed at that.

"No, airplanes got in my blood when I saw those early movies with Clark Gable and Jimmy Cagney and guys like them flying planes into weird places. You remember, those tiny little airfields surrounded by alligator-filled swamps?" Meg was quiet for a moment before she added, "You kinda remind me of Clark Gable when you put on that old leather helmet. Hey, you didn't bring that with you, did you?"

"Nah," Hal began. "Oh yeah, of course I did, and I brought one for you too." They laughed some more before turning in for the night.

THE ROOSTER FLIES HOME

BY THE TIME THEY REACHED TOKYO, the weather had shifted and a light drizzle fell throughout the first day. Meg and Hal checked over the three airports and chose one about fifty miles from Tokyo, a small field much like Harmony Field. The owner assured them, through labored translations, they would not be bothered by reporters.

Still, the two had to fight off reporters every time they came out of hiding. Word had reached Tokyo that a crazy American had arrived to fly a vintage airplane across the Pacific. After one very near encounter, Hal decided they'd better stay close to their new departure field.

The rain dragged on as June moved from the fifth day to the sixth and onto the seventh.

"We're going to have to take off in the rain if this keeps up. We have to be out of here early on the ninth," Hal observed. "It's going to be close enough as it is, with good weather."

"I promised Noah that if weather developed or we had trouble, we'd set down on one of the nearest islands. He finally approved our route since we are never very far from land at any point in the flight."

"Buck up, my pretty, the clouds will part, the rain will withdraw, and we shall have sunshine all the way home... well, except at night, of course."

Hal proved to be almost right. The rains did let up during the night of the eighth, and the morning of the ninth showed a bit of rosy sky to the east as he and Meg made their way through the deserted airfield in the land of the rising sun.

The small service crew had moved Harmony's Hope onto the tarmac and were checking it out when the pilot and navigator appeared. Hal took one side and Meg took the other to check it over again, make sure the exterior was ready for the long flight home. Once inside, they checked their gear, buttoning down anything that might move. It was all a tight squeeze, with gasoline tanks filling most of the interior.

Meg re-checked the radio before turning it off, then secured their water and food supply. Before they closed the canopy, they both leaned out and smiled for the camera held by one of the workers. It wasn't Movietone, but what the heck. There would be some record that they were taking off in Japan on June 9, 1983, exactly fifty years after Hal's infamous "takeoff" in the States.

With a spin of the propeller, Hal moved the plane to the end of the runway and let the engine roar into action. The takeoff was awkward with the load it carried. Sloshing gasoline in barrels was different from the firm hardware on the test flight. But the wheels left the field as planned and the two crazy Americans were airborne. They cheered themselves loudly over the sound of the pounding engine.

For the next two days, they chatted, if you can call it that, nudging each other and pointing outside when they spotted landmarks and such. One *such* was a jet airliner that dipped its wings as it passed them going the other way. Pilots are courteous people.

Keeping his promise to himself, Hal refused to give up the control of the plane, satisfied only with brief catnaps as Meg kept watch. She, however, enjoyed longer naps, but only when she knew he was wide awake.

Their only quarrel came on the second day when Meg thought they were lost. She gestured wildly at the maps and the instruments, unsure of readings on equipment that wasn't computerized. Hal assured her that if she was lost, then he was lost too. He motioned to the islands below, then pointed to Meg's map. The Aleutians. They were nearing home and the sun was already at the horizon, shining directly into their eyes.

When Meg pointed to the gas gauge and indicated they could get fuel on one of the islands, Hal shook his head vigorously. No! "This will be nonstop to the States," he mouthed the words to her.

"But this *is* the United States," she said as she leaned over to shout in his ear. "Remember? Alaska is a state now!"

"Humph," was Hal's response. "We have been getting some turbulence…"

"Now might be a good time to look for an island and add some weight," she coaxed. "We'd be on American soil, Hal. We've made it — across the Pacific, Japan to the U.S. without a stop in *less* than two days."

The light went on in Hal's head. "You know, I remember landing on one of the Aleuts during the war. Now what was it? Oh yes, Adak. They had Air Force units there. Where are we?"

Meg pulled out the map. When she looked up, she spotted the speck in the dawning light that coordinated with Adak. She pointed her thumb at the speck and Hal turned on the radio.

After the preliminaries, they prepared to land at the Adak Airport. "It's bigger now than it was then," Hal noted. Meg was right. The plane handled differently as the fuel load decreased, and the landing wasn't the softest ever. They needed the extra fuel, for weight if nothing else.

Officially, they were on U.S. soil; the nonstop trip had been completed. Once on the ground, they stretched their bodies before checking out the plane's exterior and securing the added fuel. Amiable islanders arrived to peer at the strange little plane and its "crazy American" pilots.

Refreshed, Meg and Hal returned to the cockpit and settled in for the last leg of their journey. While the atmospheric temperatures had been cold, the daylight sun felt warm for mid-June and they were headed for Tacoma's City Airport, Washington, in the good old U.S. of A.

All through the day, they nudged and pointed at familiar landmarks along the coast, heading southerly past Alaska and Canada. By evening, they knew they were in Washington, and soon they welcomed the glow of night lights over Tacoma. While they would have preferred to land at Harmony Field, they knew they'd have to go through customs, and the nearest customs airport, besides Sea-Tac, was in Tacoma.

"Home sweet home," Meg called out. "Isn't the city beautiful?"

Hal, working the radio, yelled, "I can't raise anybody at Harmony Field. What the… we're getting waved off Tacoma's City Airport. This isn't the right time of year for ground fog. Jumping jehosiphat! We fly five thousand miles and can't land in our own backyard."

"I told Noah we'd be due back today. It's late. Maybe he thinks we've crashed or something. What do they say is wrong with the field?"

Hal listened to his earphones for a moment, then "They say they want us to go to Sea-Tac, for customs, for crying out loud!

Like we've got any room to be carrying contraband. What the…"

"I don't understand, Hal. They can't think we're carrying drugs or something. Maybe they're going to arrest us. You know how we've avoided the FAA all along."

"Well, babe, we gotta land somewhere. The fuel is almost gone. It may as well be Sea-Tac if that's what they want. Never thought I'd be landing a plane there. Never thought I could get the clearance."

"Hal, something's not right. Noah said he'd take care of having a custom's agent on duty at Tacoma City. He said…"

"Relax, Meggie. We're home. We made it. Another couple of miles won't make a difference. We can call the kids from the airport and they can come get us. We're home. We did it! Yahoo! Cockadoodle-do!"

"Calm down. There's Sea-Tac. Is your radio on? Gee, I'm glad we decided to use it. We'd never make it down between those big jets."

"Quiet. I'm getting landing instructions… okay… roger… roger that… the main runway? What the hell? Are you crazy? I don't want to meet any of your jets plowing through there. Repeat! (pause) Hmm… are you sure? Okay, you're the boss."

"What's going on?"

"Tower says we're to go in on Number One Runway. Must be a slow night." To the radio, he said, "Roger. Taxi to Building G. Coming in."

The small yellow bird flew lower, finally touching down on Runway One. As the plane turned to taxi toward the terminal,

Meg was the first to notice crowds of people. Outside, on the tarmac. Then Hal spotted them.

"What the... blue blazes... my great Aunt Sophie!"

"Oh my god, Hal. Look at that. They're waiting for *us*, all those people. The signs. Do you see the signs? They say 'Welcome Home Hal and Meg'."

Speechless, tears streaming down his cheeks, Hal took one last glimpse at that day of infamy in 1933, remembering for the very last time the faces in that silent crowd that witnessed his devastation.

The noise of the Sea-Tac crowd rose as they closed in on Building G. They pushed back the canopy to hear the cheers and... was that a band? Banners were stretched across the tarmac. "All of Seattle and Tacoma must be out there," Hal observed.

When Harmony's Hope pulled up to the directed slot, Hal ceremoniously turned off the engine. They emerged from the plane with smiles spread across their dirty faces. They hugged each other and climbed down to the crowd that was yelling their congratulations.

Right in front were their families and co-workers, all the people who had worked to make the yellow bird fly. They easily spotted Melee, holding up a sign that read: Welcome Home, Grasshoppers.

When flash bulbs went off around them, Hal turned to see television cameras too with their bright lights — from all the Seattle stations. He blinked. "Well, I'll be. This beats Movietone News in black and white!" He took a deep breath and exhaled. "Look, Meg. Look. Over on the wing."

"It's that chicken."

"Rooster, Meg. Rooster. But look, he's on the wing. Go to war, Miss Agnes! Doodle-do flew up to the wing to greet us. How about that!"

Meg turned to Hal and grabbed his hands. "Welcome home, slugger. Who says an old rooster can't fly. You've hit a homerun!"

Hal added the last word, "You pitched it!"

They faced the crowd together. Some things remain unfinished.

15396039R00070

Made in the USA
Charleston, SC
01 November 2012